Family, Friends, and Foes

Cruise Ship Christian Cozy Mysteries Series

Book 11

Hope Callaghan

hopecallaghan.com
Copyright © 2017
All rights reserved.
***

This book is a work of fiction. Although places mentioned may be real, the characters, names and incidents and all other details are products of the author's imagination and are used fictitiously. Any resemblance to actual events or actual persons, living or dead is purely coincidental.

No part of this publication may be copied, reproduced in any format, by any means, electronic or otherwise, without prior consent from the copyright owner and publisher of this book. The only exception is brief quotations in printed reviews.

Visit my website for new releases and special offers: hopecallaghan.com

Thank you, Peggy H., Jean P., Cindi G., Wanda D. and Barbara W. for taking the time to preview *Family, Friends, and Foes,* for the extra sets of eyes and for catching all of my mistakes.

A special thanks to my reader review team: Alice, Amary, Barbara, Becky, Becky B, Brinda, Cassie, Christina, Debbie, Dee, Denota, Devan, Grace, Jan, Jo-Ann, Joeline, Joyce, Jean K., Jean M., Lynne, Megan, Melda, Kat, Linda, Lynne, Pat, Patsy, Paula, Renate, Rita, Rita P, Shelba, Tamara, Valerie and Vicki.

CONTENTS

Cast of Characters iv
Chapter 1 1
Chapter 2 10
Chapter 3 25
Chapter 4 37
Chapter 5 53
Chapter 6 73
Chapter 7 92
Chapter 8 109
Chapter 9 123
Chapter 10 137
Chapter 11 150
Chapter 12 164
Chapter 13 177
Chapter 14 201
Chapter 15 216
Chapter 16 234
Chapter 17 245
Chapter 18 258
Chapter 19 273
Chapter 20 289
Save 50-90% on Your Next Cozy Mystery......... 292
List of Hope Callaghan Books 293
Get Free eBooks and More 297
Meet the Author 298
Bacon Mac 'n Cheese Bites Recipe 299
Baked Apple and Walnut Tart Recipe 300

Cast of Characters

Mildred Sanders. Mildred "Millie" Sanders, heartbroken after her husband left her for one of his clients, decides to take a position as assistant cruise director aboard the mega cruise ship, the Siren of the Seas. From day one, she discovers she has a knack for solving mysteries, which is a good thing since some sort of crime is always being committed on the high seas.

Annette Delacroix. Director of food and beverage on board the Siren of the Seas, Annette has a secret past, which makes her the perfect accomplice in Millie's investigations. Annette is the "Jill of all Trades" and isn't afraid to roll up her sleeves and help out a friend in need.

Catherine "Cat" Wellington. Cat is the most cautious of the group of friends and prefers to help Millie from the sidelines. But when push comes to shove, Cat can be counted on to risk life and limb in the pursuit of justice.

Danielle Kneldon. Millie's cabin mate. Headstrong and gung ho, Danielle loves a good adventure and loves physical challenges, including scaling the side of the ship, scouring the jungles of Central America and working undercover to solve a mystery.

"The thief comes only to steal and kill and destroy; I have come that they may have life, and have it to the full." John 10:10 NIV

Chapter 1

Millie's heart skipped a beat as she caught a glimpse of her daughter, Beth, and family dart up the gangway. "They're here." She nudged her betrothed and jogged to the entrance, enveloping her daughter in a warm embrace.

Bella, Millie's granddaughter, tugged on the edge of her jacket. "Nana."

"Bella." Millie knelt down, wrapping one arm around Bella and the other around her grandson, Noah, pulling them close. Sudden tears burned the back of her eyes and she blinked rapidly. This was a moment she'd been looking forward to for weeks, ever since Captain Armati…Nic and she had finally set a wedding date. "I've missed you so much."

Noah lifted a pudgy hand and patted the plastic Mickey Mouse ears perched atop his head. "We went to Disney World and I saw Mickey Mouse. We camped at Fort Wilderness and even rode the fast train to the castle."

Bella nudged her brother out of the way. "I got to see the Little Mermaid and Cinderella," she said. "They're not real."

"They are too," Noah insisted.

"Are not."

"Stop," Beth warned. "We'll turn right around and leave Nana if you two don't stop fighting."

Millie's son-in-law, David, rolled his eyes. "I swear we had the longest four hour drive south. Traffic on I-95 was horrible. The closer we got to Miami, the worse it got."

"But it was worth it," Beth insisted.

"Of course."

Millie turned as someone nearby tapped her on the shoulder. "Yes?"

"How long will the lunch buffet be open?" a passenger asked.

Millie glanced at her watch. "Until 3:30, when the ship sets sail and the mandatory safety briefing, also known as the muster drill, starts."

The woman thanked her before walking away.

"We should let you get back to work," Beth gave her husband a quick glance. "Before we go, I have something I need to give you."

David cleared his throat. "Kids, let's go check out our cabin." He gave his wife a peck on the cheek and Millie could've sworn he whispered "good luck" under his breath.

Danielle, Millie's friend and another of the cruise ship's entertainment staff, joined the women. "I can handle the crowds if you need a brief break."

"Thanks Danielle," Millie smiled gratefully and then turned to her daughter. "What's up? I can tell by the look on your face that something's going on."

"There is...sort of." Beth began wringing her hands and giving her mother an 'I-would-rather-be-anywhere-but-here look.'

Millie motioned her daughter off to the side. "Are you upset that Captain Armati and I are marrying?" Her daughter had seemed thrilled at the thought that her mother had found love again, especially after Roger, Millie's ex-husband and Beth's father, left her for another woman, one of his clients, no less.

Roger's betrayal had been the catalyst for Millie to change her life, to apply for the job as assistant cruise director aboard the Siren of the Seas, which is where she'd met Captain Armati.

"No." Beth shook her head. "I'm thrilled you're happy. Just look at you Mom. You're positively glowing."

"Then what's up? Did Blake change his mind and decide not to come?" Blake, Millie's son, was more of a homebody. He would rather be out in the woods hunting or on the river fishing. But Blake seemed excited for his mother and the fact that he'd agreed to come on the cruise and the first leg of the ship's sailing was one of the best wedding gifts Millie could hope for.

"No. Blake called me from the airport. He and Erin are on the way."

Millie had yet to meet Erin, Blake's new girlfriend. She'd asked for her daughter's take on Erin, but all Beth would say was she wanted her mother to form her own opinion.

Although the original plan was for Nic and Millie to marry in Miami and then honeymoon at another location, all of that changed when one of Nic's closest friends, Regan Leclerc, offered to let them stay at his all-inclusive, five star resort on the island of Saint-Martin as a wedding present. He even offered a couple of free nights for Millie and Nic's children.

The place sounded fabulous. The couple could rest and relax with little travel, and the Siren of the Seas would pick them up the following week.

Ted Danvers, CEO of Majestic Cruise Lines, had agreed to allow the ship to switch itineraries, so that their honeymoon location would be the first port stop.

It would work out perfectly. The wedding was the following day, Sunday, and Millie's family, as well as Captain Armati's daughter, Fiona, all planned to disembark in Saint-Martin where they would catch a flight back to Miami the following day.

"It's something else." Beth reached into her purse and pulled out an envelope. Millie's name was scrawled on the front and the handwriting looked familiar.

"What's this?" Millie took the envelope from her daughter.

"It's a letter from Dad."

Millie immediately tried to hand it back, but Beth shook her head. "I promised Dad I would give you this note as soon as we boarded the ship. He told me if I didn't promise to hand it to you, he was going to book a cabin and join us."

The color drained from Millie's face. "He wouldn't dare," she whispered. Visions of her ex-husband storming onto the ship and causing a scene raced through Millie's mind. "Does he still think I'm responsible for Delilah's death?"

"No. He knows you had nothing to do with that." Beth shifted her feet. "He's been acting differently since Delilah died. He calls me almost every day, wants to spend more time with Noah and Bella. He even bought birthday presents for them this year, without me having to remind him."

"Maybe he wants to apologize," Beth said.

"There's only one way to find out." Millie removed the single sheet of paper from the envelope and began reading:

"My Dearest Millie,

First, let me say that I'm sorry for the hurt I have caused you. I know an apology now, after all of this time, will do little to heal the pain.

Not many can live with the idea of being cheated upon. Not many can put the past behind them and revive a troubled relationship. Not many can find it in their heart to find happiness in a man who betrayed their deepest trust. I understand that perfectly. The wound in your heart requires time to heal and it is only right that I allowed you the space to do so.

This relationship of ours is now at a crossroad. But I know that the decision of where we go from here is not mine to make. I relinquished my right when I cheated on you.

I have done so much soul-searching these last few months and have come to the realization that I can't live without you. I'm begging you, Millie, to give me one more chance.

Please, for the sake of our children, for the sake of our grandchildren, postpone your wedding. You – we – deserve a second chance. I still love you and wish fervently for a chance for our relationship to bloom once again.

I'm waiting outside in the cruise port, hoping and praying you'll come out and talk to me. Please Millie, I'm begging you, to at least spare a few moments of your time before you make the biggest mistake of your life...marrying a man you barely know.

Love – Roger."

Millie reached out to steady herself as she teetered between the urge to throw up and laugh hysterically. Instead, she carefully folded the note. "Your father is outside, waiting for me to come out and talk to him."

Beth's eyes widened. "You're kidding. He *promised* me he wouldn't do that. I had no idea. You're not going to go, are you?"

Millie sucked in a breath. "Actually, I think I will."

Chapter 2

Something wasn't quite right and it needed to be better than right…it needed to be perfect. The killer stepped lightly along the edge of the Jacuzzi tub as he studied the body.

It was a pity, really. It had almost been hard to kill the blonde woman. She was funny, engaging…rich. He stared at the large diamond ring on her right hand and thought about removing the gem and slipping it into his pocket, but then it would no longer be the perfect murder.

There would be evidence. The last thing he needed, couldn't afford, was a careless act, a clue for the authorities to track the murder…murders, to him. No. The gem wasn't worth the risk.

Instead, he slipped a gloved hand under the woman's left arm and gently lifted it, so that it rested near her head.

Next, he lifted her right arm, propping her elbow on the bath pillow as he placed the palm of her hand across her mouth before straightening his back. Now it was perfect. "Two down, three to go," he rasped.

The killer silently stepped out of the bathroom. He looked back one final time before slipping out of the hotel room and vanishing into the cool Caribbean morning air.

***

Millie tucked the note in her pocket and made her way across the atrium where Danielle stood greeting the boarding guests. "I need to make a quick trip to the dock to talk to Roger."

Danielle lifted a brow. "Roger as in your ex-husband Roger?"

"Yes. He wrote me a letter of apology and now he's waiting outside the cruise terminal. He wants to talk."

"About what?" Danielle asked bluntly. "What an idiot and loser he is? What if he wants you to reconcile?"

"He does."

"And you're going to meet him? *Are you nuts*?" Danielle hissed.

"I'm not nuts," Millie said stiffly. "At least I hope I'm not nuts."

"What are you gonna say? 'Gee Roger. I'm glad you came to your senses before it was too late and I marry the hottest man I've ever met in my life and live happily ever after.'"

Despite the seriousness of the matter, Millie grinned. "I detect a hint of sarcasm."

"It's more than a hint." Danielle paused. "You're going to go talk to him?"

"I am and I'll be back in less than half an hour."

"You better be alone," Danielle said.

Millie shook her head, but didn't reply as she strode down the gangway. When she reached the docking area, she circled around to the side exit marked, *Restricted Access: Crew and Staff Only*. She flashed her badge at the port security guard and then made a beeline for the sidewalk out front.

The terminal staging area was a madhouse as hordes of passengers handed their luggage to waiting porters and searched for their designated boarding line.

Millie paused long enough to answer a couple of quick questions from harried soon-to-be guests and then wandered along the sidewalk before crossing the busy street.

She slowly made her way around the perimeter of the docking area, searching for her ex-husband. Perhaps Roger had changed his mind and wasn't there after all. She stepped into the crosswalk and then caught a glimpse of a familiar figure, standing next to a bench and facing the other way.

Millie slowly made her way to the bench. "Hello Roger."

Roger spun around. "Millie." He smiled hesitantly. "I wasn't sure if you would show."

She said the first thing that popped into her head. "You tricked Beth."

"I had to. She would never have delivered my note if she knew I was going to be here."

"You're wasting your time," Millie said. "I…"

"I'm not wasting my time. I'm here because I think you're rushing into this marriage. You don't know Captain Alcati very well." Roger hurried on. "Yes, I admit I made a mistake…a big mistake and I'm willing to admit it, but I've had plenty of time to think about what I've done." Roger reached for Millie's hand and she took a quick step back.

"Think about us, Millie. We have history. We have a beautiful family. We have grandchildren. Let's start over," Roger pleaded. "I can sell the business. We can travel, like we always talked about."

"First of all, his name is Armati. Captain Niccolo Armati." It was Millie's turn to cut her ex off. "Roger, you cheated on me. You nearly destroyed me, but you didn't. In fact, your selfish, careless act made me strong…stronger than I've ever been. I'm happy, happier now than I ever could've imagined. I've met someone I love deeply and he loves me."

"What about your family? We miss you. It's time to come home."

Millie slowly shook her head as she stared at the man she had married and loved for so many years. All she felt now was pity. "I forgive you, Roger. I forgive you for what you put me through."

She waved her hand toward the Siren of the Seas. "This is my home. This is my life. I will always have my children and grandchildren; I'm just not able to see them as often as I would like. It's over,

Roger. It was over a long time ago." Millie turned to go, before slowly turning back. "Oh, and the part about wanting to travel? I think I've got that covered."

Without saying another word, Millie straightened her back and slowly made her way across the street, to the Siren of the Seas...her home, and it felt good, as if a weight had been lifted from her shoulders, once and for all.

Beth, who was still inside the atrium when Millie returned, crossed the room when she spotted her mother. "Was Dad really out there? What did you say to him?"

"He was there. He told me I needed to give him a second chance," Millie said. "He also said he would sell Central Michigan Private Investigators, retire and we could travel."

"He did?" Beth's eyes widened.

"Yes, and I told him I've got it covered," Millie said.

Beth pressed a hand to her chest. "I am so sorry Mom. I had no idea."

"Your father told me that." Millie squeezed her daughter's arm. "It's okay. Honestly, it's a relief. It feels as if a weight has been lifted off of me."

Beth nodded to Danielle, who now stood next to Andy, the Siren of the Seas Cruise Director and Millie's boss. "Andy stopped by to say 'hi' and asked where you were."

"I better get back to work," Millie said.

"We'll catch up with you later." Beth gave her mom a quick hug and then disappeared inside one of the elevators while Millie crossed the atrium and joined Andy and Danielle.

"I take it you put out whatever fire Danielle was talking about?" Andy asked.

"Yep." Millie nodded firmly. "It's completely extinguished."

A group of passengers wandered over and Millie quickly shifted into assistant cruise director mode. Summer was in full swing and Andy had told the staff earlier, during their morning meeting, that the ship was booked to capacity.

Despite it being hurricane season, it was also the busiest time of the year, with families taking advantage of children being out of school. Millie secretly preferred the fall months, when the weather was a little cooler.

Andy waited until there was a lull in the crowd. "Fiona, Captain Armati's daughter, boarded while you were gone."

"Rats." Millie had hoped to be one of the first to welcome Fiona on board the ship. "My timing is impeccable." She had no idea what to expect of Nic's daughter. The two were close and from little tidbits Millie was able to glean, Fiona had been especially close to her mother, who had died in a car accident while Nic was at sea.

She remembered Nic telling her Fiona was angry with her father for not being there when Lisa, his wife, died. They had worked through Fiona's anger and she wondered what Fiona thought of her father remarrying.

Millie wished she'd been able to meet Fiona before the wedding, but their schedules were so hectic, there was no time to squeeze in a trip to Bertoli, where his daughter, divorced and childless, lived. "I wonder if I missed my son, Blake, and his girlfriend, Erin."

"This place has been a madhouse," Danielle said. "I probably wouldn't have noticed him even if I knew what he looked like."

Millie pressed both hands to her cheeks, praying Blake and Erin would make it on board before the ship set sail. Between Roger writing her letters, begging her to reconcile with him, not to mention the stress of meeting Nic's only child, Fiona, and Blake's girlfriend, Erin, she was beginning to think she wouldn't survive the next 24-hours, long enough for Pastor Evans to perform the ceremony.

"Why don't you take a break," Andy suggested. "You can run up to the lido deck to make sure the sail away party is running smoothly."

Millie nodded. "If you don't mind. I'm wound up tighter than a top."

Andy gave Millie a quick hug. "As any bride-to-be, hours away from walking down the aisle, should be."

"If you're trying to make me feel better, it's not working," Millie joked. She thanked Andy for the break and ascended the stairs on the other side of the atrium.

Millie slipped into her routine as she made her rounds, picking up a small stack of dirty dishes, a few empty drink glasses and dropping them in the bin near the bar.

She made a quick trip through the buffet area and to the pool in the back before climbing two more sets of stairs where she found herself standing in front of the Sky Chapel.

The urge to spend a few quiet moments alone was tempting, and Millie made her way into the sanctuary where she slid onto an empty pew in the back. The last few days of preparing for not only a wedding, but also a honeymoon and planning time with family, had taken their toll. Millie hadn't slept well in days.

She rested her arm on the pew in front of her and placed her forehead on top as she prayed for peace and calm. She prayed Fiona would like her and that the wedding would go off without a hitch. Millie even prayed for Roger, that he would find happiness like she had.

Squeak. Millie jerked her head and watched as Pastor Pete made his way to the back of the chapel. "I thought I saw someone sneak in here." He eased into the pew in front of Millie. "Are you all right? You're not getting cold feet, are you?"

"No." Millie smiled. "I needed a breather. In between the wedding, the honeymoon, family and work, not to mention a surprise visit from my ex-husband, I'm feeling a little stressed out."

"Oh dear," the pastor said. "Your ex-husband isn't on board the ship again, is he?"

"No. Thank heavens. He was outside waiting for me," Millie said. "I think he's gone now."

Pastor Pete nodded. "Have you met Fiona yet?"

"No. I missed her. I'm nervous she won't like me," Millie confessed. "Have you met her?"

"Yes. I met her a couple of years ago, during her last visit."

"Do you think she'll like me?" Millie asked.

Pastor Pete studied Millie's face. "I don't know her well enough to be able to answer your question, Millie. She took her mother's death very hard and blamed her father for a long time. It's hard to say. She may like you right away or it may take some time for her to appreciate what a wonderful, warm person you are."

"So you're saying she probably won't," Millie groaned.

"No. I'm saying you have a 50/50 chance."

"Millie do you copy?" Millie's radio squawked. It was Andy.

She plucked the radio from her belt and pressed the side button. "Go ahead Andy."

"I need you to meet me in the bridge as soon as possible."

"I'm on my way." Millie clipped her radio to her belt and scrambled to her feet. "Great. Now what?"

"I'm sure it's nothing." Pastor Pete stood. "See you tomorrow?"

"I sure hope so," Millie said before she exited the chapel. "Just keep praying."

When she reached the bridge, Millie tapped lightly on the door and swiped her card before stepping inside. Her heart sank when she saw not only Andy, but Captain Armati, Captain Vitale and

Danielle huddled near the center of the room. "What's going on?"

Nic broke from the group and hurried to Millie's side. "I spoke with my friend, Regan, who owns Grand Bay Beach Club, where we planned to honeymoon."

"Is everything all right?"

"He wanted to give me a heads up. There have been a couple of unexpected tragedies."

"What kind of tragedies?"

"One of the front desk clerks was found dead a couple of days ago and then this morning, a guest's body was found inside one of the hotel rooms."

Chapter 3

"Oh dear. How awful," Millie said. "Maybe we should cancel our honeymoon."

"The decision is up to us." Nic squeezed Millie's hand. "Regan said we don't have to, but wanted me to know what was going on. What do you think?"

"A dead body or two never stopped Millie before," Andy quipped.

Millie shot him a dark look.

"It's too late to plan another honeymoon," Nic explained. "We could postpone it."

"It was like pulling teeth trying to get this next week off. It might be another year before we get a honeymoon if we postpone it now." Millie began to pace. On the one hand, she didn't want to appear callous to Regan's crisis, but she also didn't want to miss out on their honeymoon. "I say we go ahead with our plans."

"Perfect." Nic beamed. "That's my girl." The smile vanished. "Promise me you won't try to turn the deaths into some sort of mystery."

"What on earth makes you think I would do something like that?"

Danielle snorted. "C'mon Millie. I'll bet you a month of hosting the behind the scenes tours you'll somehow become involved."

"It's a deal." Millie's least favorite task was taking the guests on the tour. It wasn't because she didn't enjoy interacting with them. It was just they sometimes asked questions she couldn't answer...like how many rolls of toilet paper housekeeping went through in a week. "I plan to spend the entire time resting, relaxing and enjoying the company of my husband."

"Well, that settles it," Captain Vitale said. "We'll carry on with our plans as is, dropping both of you and your families off in Philipsburg and then picking you two up during our port stop the following week."

"Good. Let's get back to work," Andy said.

"It's time for me to head down to the ship lobby tour," Danielle said.

"And I'm on my way to the island excursion chat in the Kickstart Comedy Den." Millie trailed behind Andy and Danielle as they made their way out of the bridge.

"Hold up, Millie," Captain Armati said. "I need to talk to you for a moment."

"See you later." Millie waited for Andy and Danielle to exit the bridge before Captain Armati and she walked to the other side of the room.

"I'll check on the loading progress." Captain Vitale stepped out onto the bridge deck.

Nic waited until the door closed behind Vitale. "Danielle mentioned something about you exiting the ship earlier."

"Yes. I almost forgot." Millie plucked Roger's note from her pocket and handed it to Nic. He silently unfolded the paper and read the brief letter before folding it back up and handing it to Millie. "Roger showed up here?"

"Yes." Millie nodded. "I told him I forgave him for everything he put me through and wished him the best. I think he's clear on my feelings towards him. If not for him, I wouldn't have my children and two beautiful grandchildren."

"True. We have enough going on right now without having him board the ship and causing us any more stress than we already have," Nic said. "Speaking of stress, Fiona arrived a short time ago. I showed her to her cabin and she's resting now."

"Is she feeling ill?"

"She'll be fine." Nic shook his head. "It was a long flight, and she's suffering from jetlag. We're going to be busy the rest of the day, so I told her we would catch up at dinner tonight. She's joining us at the captain's table, along with your children. Has your son, Blake, and his girlfriend arrived?"

"Beth said they were on the way. I guess I'll get to meet Blake's girlfriend, Erin, this evening too." Millie shook her head. "Hopefully, after today, things will calm down."

"Until the wedding tomorrow." Nic pulled Millie into his arms and lowered his head as he gently kissed her lips.

A surge of heat ran through Millie's veins and for a moment, she forgot about her children, forgot about Nic's daughter and the upcoming wedding ceremony.

Finally, Nic pulled away, a smoldering dark look in his eyes. "Maybe we should move the wedding up to today."

"Kiss me like that again and we just might." Millie reluctantly glanced at her watch. "I need to get going. I'm sure the guests are wondering what happened to their excursion host." She bounced up on her tiptoes to give her betrothed one more quick kiss and then strode to the door before she could change her mind.

The ship had switched itineraries and Millie wasn't familiar with the new ports and activities. Thankfully, she'd jotted down some notes on the shore excursions and had even remembered to bring them with her.

Millie slipped past several passengers as she made her way to the small stage. She switched the stage mic on and smiled at the guests. "Welcome aboard Siren of the Seas. My name is Millie and I'm the ship's assistant cruise director. How many of you have cruised on the Siren of the Seas before?"

After the icebreaker, Millie rolled into her presentation and by the time she finished the hour-long presentation, she was proud of herself for being able to answer the majority of the passengers' questions, most of which related to the ship and onboard activities, and not the ports.

Several of the excursions sounded intriguing, including a taste of the island tour for both the French and Dutch sides. Millie also decided the sunset catamaran cruise sounded romantic.

After the last passenger departed, she flipped the lights off and closed the door behind her. Her next stop was to swing by the ship's gift shop to make sure Cat was ready for the wedding the following day.

Millie had asked her friends Cat, Danielle and Annette to stand up with her and she wanted to remind them of the 3:00 wedding.

The gift shop was packed and a large display sign near the entrance touted the Welcome Aboard Jewelry Blowout Sale. She caught a glimpse of Cat, who was helping a customer at the jewelry counter and decided to keep going.

Her next stop was the galley. Millie peeked inside the door and caught a glimpse of Annette and Amit, standing in front of the prep station. She could tell from the look on her friend's face they were in the midst of a serious discussion.

"This is brilliant Amit." Annette patted her right-hand man's arm. "I never thought to use extra sharp cheddar cheese. It gives these an extra tang. Good job."

Millie crept up behind them. "What? Amit did something right this time?" she teased.

Amit shifted to the side, his face beaming. "Miss Millie. Would you like to sample one of your wedding hors d'oeuvres?"

"Ooh. What is it?" Annette had refused to tell Millie what she planned to serve for the cocktail party reception, only telling her she'd hand-picked the special dishes as a wedding gift for the couple.

"They're bite-size bacon wrapped mac 'n cheese treats. My recipe called for cheddar cheese and Amit decided to step it up a notch by using extra sharp cheddar instead. Try one." Annette lifted one of the appetizers from the muffin pan and held it out. "It's still a little hot, so be careful."

Millie's mouth watered as she eyed the crispy bacon and caramelized breadcrumbs coating the cheesy pasta goodness. She took a small bite and a string of cheese hung from a macaroni shell. She pulled it loose with her finger and popped it into her mouth. "Oh my gosh. This is delicious." She polished off the rest of the treat and eyed the muffin pan. "I want this recipe."

"It's super easy," Annette said. "All you need is bacon, macaroni shells, milk, butter, extra sharp cheddar cheese and breadcrumbs."

"Sometimes the easiest recipes are the best," Amit said.

"You're absolutely right. I better try one more, just to make sure." Millie plucked another goody from the tray and took a big bite.

Annette reached for another tray on the other side of Amit. "Since you didn't want a traditional wedding cake, we stuck with the theme of small dishes. "Try this." She held out a tiered tray of golden brown pastry tarts.

"These look delicious. What are they?"

"Baked apple and walnut tarts, fresh from the oven."

Millie took a small bite of the tart. A savory hint of cinnamon, mixed with brown sugar, melted in her mouth. "I taste cinnamon."

"Just a pinch." Annette pinched her thumb and index finger together. "I'm going to serve them with a side of heavy whipped cream and confectioners' sugar."

"Perfect." Millie gave a thumbs-up. "You two outdid yourselves. These are the bomb."

"I'm glad you like them, Miss Millie," Amit said. "The wedding, it will be beautiful."

"Thanks Amit. I can't wait until it's over."

Amit wandered to the dessert station and Millie waited until he was out of earshot. "Roger talked Beth into delivering a note to me when she boarded the ship." Millie explained to her friend what had happened. "Now that it's over, I'm glad I went out there to talk to Roger. Our marriage ended on such a horrible note. The air is finally clear and I had my say. I can finally close that chapter of my life and move on."

"It's good you're able to see the bright side," Annette shook her head. "Still, I think he's a jerk for trying to pull something like that at the last moment. Does Captain Armati know?"

"Yeah. I let him read the note and told him what I said. Roger even went as far as to promise me he would sell the business and we could travel."

Annette grunted. "Did you let him know you've got that part covered?"

"You took the words right out of my mouth, which reminds me, there have been a couple of deaths over at Grand Bay Beach Club, the resort where we're honeymooning," Millie said.

"Recently?"

"In the last couple of days," Millie said. "I don't know any of the details yet."

"A mystery. That's right up your alley." Annette stuck a fist on her hip. "Ten bucks says you'll be sleuthing on your honeymoon."

"You sound like Danielle."

"It's in your blood, Millie." Annette changed the subject. "Have you met Blake's girlfriend yet?"

"No. I still have a few minutes left of my break. I was thinking of stopping by his cabin to see if they've boarded yet." Millie blinked rapidly as she gazed at the food her friend had prepared for her special day. "Thanks for everything Annette. You're the best friend I've ever had."

"Same here," Annette said. "Now get out of here before you have both of us bawling like babies."

Chapter 4

Millie checked to make sure that the *Do Not Disturb* light was off before she tapped lightly on Blake's cabin door. When no one answered, she turned to go. The door opened a crack.

"Blake?"

The door opened wider and a petite, brown-haired woman appeared in the doorway. "Blake ran upstairs to get some pop."

"Are you Erin?"

"Yes." Erin gazed at Millie's name tag. "You're Blake's mother."

"Yes. I'm Millie." She smiled and extended a hand. "It's so nice to finally meet you."

"Same here. Blake talks about you all of the time. Why, the day we met...did Blake tell you we met on a blind date?"

Erin didn't give Millie a chance to reply. In fact, she didn't even stop to take a breath as she continued. "Well, not technically a blind date. Blake's friend, Mick, introduced us. It was more of a double date. Blake was so sweet. He held the door for me. We found out on our very first date we have a lot in common. Blake likes to hunt. I like to hunt. I love venison. I have this wonderful recipe for venison stew."

Erin frowned. "Although I'm not sure they serve venison on a cruise ship." She shrugged. "I suppose you could always use ground beef instead of venison."

Erin rattled on while Millie tried hard to keep up with all of the information Erin was divulging. She learned that the young woman was the youngest sibling in a large family, and the family owned a dairy farm north of Grand Rapids.

She also discovered Erin worked as a veterinarian's assistant and was finishing her education to become a vet.

Millie felt a light tug on her sleeve; she spun around and faced her son. "Blake." She hugged him tight; all the while Erin continued talking, never once stopping.

"I see you and Erin have met."

"Yes. She was telling me about..." Millie's voice trailed off.

"Everything," Blake prompted.

"Yes. A little of everything."

Blake handed the cans of soda he was carrying to Erin. "There should be some ice in the bucket."

"There is. Our room steward, Bayan, stopped by while you were gone and filled the bucket." Erin backed into the cabin. "I told him we like lots of ice and he said no problem. He also asked what time we usually get up so he wouldn't disturb us, then he showed me the cool *Do Not Disturb* light. Have you seen it?"

"Not yet." Blake turned to his mother. "I stopped by Beth and David's cabin on my way back here.

Beth told me about Dad's note and how he was out in the port area, waiting to talk to you."

"Yes. We had a brief chat. I'm sorry he's taking my upcoming wedding to Captain Armati hard. Life is full of regrets."

"I feel sorry for Dad, too, but he made his choice when he hooked up with Delilah. Now, onto more pleasant topics. Erin and I can't wait to meet Captain Armati."

"Nic. You'll meet him this evening at dinner." Millie glanced at her watch. "It's almost time for the mandatory safety drill, which means I need to go." She hugged her son a second time, catching a whiff of his cologne. "You smell nice."

"It's a new cologne called Tumbleweed," Erin handed Blake a glass of Coke. "I like it because it's not overpowering. Just the right scent. I can't wait to explore the ship. I saw on the television that we have life jackets in our cabin, but we don't have to take them to the safety briefing."

"No, you do not. I'll let you two get ready for the safety drill." Millie smiled at the couple and headed down the hall. She could still hear Erin's excited chatter until she reached the stairwell.

The rest of the afternoon flew by. After the safety briefing and the ship set sail for Sint Maarten / Saint-Martin, Millie darted from the Win a Suite bingo to the Solo Travelers Social and finally the *Welcome Aboard Show*.

Now that Andy was back from his emergency break to care for his mother, Millie could hang out on the sidelines and enjoy the show. After it ended, she stopped by her cabin to change for the captain's dinner and then headed to the *Blue Seas,* the ship's main dining room.

When she reached the entrance, she paused briefly, peeking around the corner to see if she could catch a glimpse of the table where she, along with Beth, David, Blake, Erin, Nic and his daughter, Fiona, would be dining...and meeting for the first time. From her vantage point, the only person visible was Nic.

Millie rubbed her damp palms on the front of her new sundress and cleared her throat before stepping into the room. She zigzagged around the tables as she made her way to the back, smiling and nodding at several familiar faces.

When she reached the table, she saw everyone was there...everyone except for Fiona.

Nic sprang from his seat and placed a light hand under her elbow as he led her to an empty chair. He waited for her to ease into it before sliding it in.

"Sorry if I'm late." Millie reached for her dinner napkin.

"You're right on time."

Millie's heart skipped a beat as she met Nic's gaze and realized in less than a day they would be husband and wife. She glanced around the table, her eyes resting on the vacant chair. "Fiona isn't here."

"She...uh. She's still feeling under the weather from the long flight and asked me to apologize, but she won't be making it to dinner."

"I hope she'll be all right," Millie said.

"I hope so too." Nic quickly changed the subject, inquiring about Millie's children and their trip. Beth told him the family spent several days prior to arriving at the port at Disney World, visiting the various parks and staying at Disney's campground before Erin monopolized the rest of the evening's conversation.

By the time Millie's baked chicken and grilled asparagus arrived, she'd unintentionally tuned out her son's girlfriend as her mind wandered to the wedding the following day and the deaths at Regan Leclerc's resort.

"...right Mom?" Beth asked.

Millie shook her head. "I'm sorry Beth. My mind was wandering."

"I'm sure you're thinking of the wedding," Blake said.

"Among other things," Millie murmured.

Nic shook his finger at Millie. "I recognize the look in your eyes. You're mulling over the deaths at Regan's resort."

"Deaths," Beth gasped. "Someone died?"

"An employee and a guest at the Grand Bay Beach Club, the place where we'll be staying in Saint-Martin," Millie said. "Unfortunately, we don't have the details."

Nic shifted in his seat. "I talked to Regan right before I came down here to let him know we would still be arriving on Monday, as scheduled, and he gave me some additional information."

Millie turned, giving Nic her full attention. "And?"

"The police took Regan in for questioning, but released him. He thinks the authorities are going to try to pin the deaths on him and his wife, Nadia."

"Oh dear. I suppose it would be suspect since both people died while on their property," Millie said. "What did Regan tell you?"

"The first victim was a front desk clerk. One of the hotel staff found his body in the kitchen's walk-in freezer."

Millie shivered at the thought. "He froze to death?"

"It appears so."

"What a terrible way to die," Erin said. "I remember the snowstorm we had last December. I was driving my car from Allegan back to Grand Rapids…"

Blake pressed a finger to Erin's lips. "Hang on dear. I want to hear what happened to the other person before we get sidetracked."

Erin clamped her lips together and frowned at Blake.

"What happened to the other person...the hotel guest?" Beth asked.

"It was a woman. Her husband found her body in the bathtub. She'd been strangled."

Millie's hand flew to her throat. "How awful."

"There is one more thing," Nic said. He glanced around the table and lowered his voice. "The killer posed the second body. He placed one hand over her mouth and lifted two fingers on her other hand."

"Number two," Millie whispered. "I wonder if there's a serial killer stalking the resort."

"I wondered the same thing," Nic said. "We still have time to change our minds."

Millie glanced around the table. The last thing she wanted to do was to put her children and grandchildren in harm's way. If something happened to one of them...to any of them, she would never forgive herself. "What do you think? We can see if there are any flights available, departing the island on Monday, as soon as the ship docks in Philipsburg."

"I don't want to cancel our plans." David turned to Beth. "What do you think, honey?"

"I'm with you," Beth said. "What are the chances of this happening again or something happening to one of us? No. I vote for keeping the original plan."

"Me too," Blake said. "Erin?"

Erin gazed at the others seated at the table. "I guess I'm okay with it. As long as I don't wander off by myself. I've heard stories about foreigners getting murdered on islands by locals who are poor and looking to rob unsuspecting tourists. Just last week..."

"Perfect," Blake said. "We're fine with sticking to the original plan."

"As long as Millie, your mother, doesn't make it her mission to solve the murder and look into the employee's death, we'll be all set," Nic teased.

"Don't tempt me," Millie shot back.

"You know I'm teasing," Nic said. "On a less serious note, the weather is going to be perfect with low humidity and plenty of sunshine. Since we'll all be at the resort for the first day, I thought we could plan a day together. Regan suggested maybe giving paddle boarding or shore fishing a go."

"It sounds perfect." Beth clasped her hands. "The kids love to fish."

"I was stung once by a jellyfish while vacationing in Florida. It hurt like the dickens," Erin said. "The beach was full of them." Erin rattled on while the server and his assistant returned to remove the dinner plates before handing each of them a dessert menu.

Millie shook her head. "I'm going to stick with a cup of coffee for dessert."

Beth studied the menu. "The chocolate melting cake sounds tempting."

"Good choice," Millie said. "It's served warm with a side of vanilla bean ice cream."

"Sold." Beth pointed at David. "I'm sure my husband, the chocoholic, will want to try it. We'll each have one."

"Make it three," Blake said.

"Count me in. I love chocolate," Erin handed the menu to the server. "Coffee sounds good too."

"I'm going to make this easy, Sanun." Captain Armati handed the server the dessert menu. "I'll have the melting cake, as well."

"Very good Captain Armati." Sanun bowed and backed away from the table.

Millie sipped her coffee, enjoying the light banter at the table as she waited for the others to finish their dessert.

Beth scooped the last bite of chocolate into her mouth and then licked the spoon. "We better head up to the kids camp to pick up Bella and Noah. It's been a long day and I'm sure they're getting cranky." She circled the table and hugged her mother. "We'll see you tomorrow."

"We're gonna head out too." Blake wiped the corners of his mouth and dropped his napkin on the table.

"Have fun." Millie waited until her family left the table and was out of earshot before turning to Nic. "Is Fiona really feeling under the weather?" She asked softly.

Nic lowered his gaze. "She's struggling with me getting remarried. I think the upcoming wedding brought back some memories of Lisa's death and it hit Fiona harder than she thought it would. I hope she makes it to the wedding, but I can't promise she'll be there."

"I see." Millie briefly closed her eyes and prayed for Fiona, for all of them. She opened them. "I'm sure it's difficult for her. Fiona sees so little of you and now you're bringing someone new into her life. She must see me as someone else for her to compete with."

"I love Fiona with all my heart. She's my daughter. I understand her feelings. I loved Lisa and I still feel a sliver of guilt over not being there when Lisa died and I wasn't there for my daughter."

"Not because you didn't want to be," Millie pointed out.

"That's true, but it doesn't change things." Nic's shoulders sagged. "It may take some time, but if Fiona will give you a chance, she'll love you as much as I do."

"Or at least like me," Millie said.

"Yes. Like you." Nic stood. "We better get out of here. There's still a few hours of work left and we have a big day tomorrow."

"Yes, we do." Millie led the way out of the dining room and to the nearest stairwell where Nic pulled her into an alcove and kissed her. "That was a small taste of what's to come," he said huskily.

"Tomorrow can't get here quick enough," Millie replied breathlessly. "Thankfully, I have enough to do tonight to keep me distracted."

She waited for Nic to step into the elevator before slowly making her way to the cabin to change back into her work clothes. She still had another shift to work, which included making her rounds to the comedy show and the piano bar. Her last stop would be checking in on the late night karaoke.

Millie stopped in front of the cabin door and slipped off her lanyard when the door flew open and Danielle ran through the doorway, nearly colliding with her as she dashed into the hall. "Millie, I was just coming to track you down. We have a big problem!"

Chapter 5

"I'm already on issue overload," Millie groaned. "Now what?"

"Follow me." Danielle motioned her inside their cabin and to Millie's closet. "It's your wedding dress. I promised to let you borrow my baby blue pumps for the something borrowed, something blue tradition. I was going to set them inside your closet when I smelled something funky. Check it out."

Danielle opened the closet door while Millie stuck her head inside and sniffed the air. It smelled like a sweaty locker room. "Ugh. What in the world?"

"Look up." Danielle pointed at the corner of the closet and a small vent, something Millie had never noticed before. "The smell is coming from the vent. I was gonna take your dress out of the closet and put it in mine, but mine is crammed full. I'm afraid the dress will wrinkle. We could hang it in the shower."

"Good idea." Millie carefully pulled the hanger from the rod and carried the dress to the bathroom. "But what about showering in the morning?"

"We can put it on the bed once we're up," Danielle said. "How was the big family dinner? What do you think of Captain Armati's daughter?"

"I didn't meet her. She was feeling under the weather."

"What a shame," Danielle closed the bathroom door and flipped the light off. "What about Blake's girlfriend?"

"Erin is very sweet and Blake seems to like her." Millie didn't mention she was a chatterbox and silently reminded herself there were a million things worse...like refusing to attend your father's wedding.

She forced Fiona from her mind. "I better get back into work clothes and start my rounds."

Danielle exited the cabin while Millie quickly changed. By the time she finished her shift, her feet were sore, her back ached and her nerves were frayed from worrying about the upcoming wedding, not to mention a nagging uneasiness over the recent deaths at Grand Bay Beach Club.

An isolated incident was one thing, but the fact that one of the deaths was a resort employee and the other a resort guest was disturbing.

Millie peeled off her work uniform and pulled on her pajamas before crawling into her bunk. It would be her last night sleeping alone, her last night of sharing a cabin with Danielle.

She clasped her hands and prayed that God would protect her family, would bless her marriage and that the upcoming wedding and honeymoon would be smooth sailing.

Danielle hadn't returned by the time Millie drifted off to sleep and her last thought was to wonder if

Nic snored, or if he was a cover hog. A small smile lifted the corners of her mouth and she fell into a dreamless sleep.

***

"Wake up sleeping beauty. It's your wedding day," Danielle sing-songed in Millie's ear.

Millie's eyes flew open and she blinked rapidly. "Wh-what time is it?"

"Time to get up," Danielle said. "We still have to put in a full shift before the nuptials and par-tay start."

"Are you taking the sunrise stride or the sunrise stretch?" Millie threw back the covers and wiggled out of her bunk.

"Today is all about you," Danielle said. "My wedding present is that you get to pick your schedule."

"I thought your presence as a bridesmaid was my present."

"I'm feeling particularly generous today, so I'm giving you more than one gift."

"You won't hear me complain. I'll take the sunrise stride." Millie grabbed the day's Cruise Ship Chronicles off the desk and scanned the schedule. "Then I'll host the scavenger hunt at 10:30, followed by the ballroom dancing class at 11:30."

"What about the singles Mix & Mingle?" Danielle asked.

"I'll take that, too, since you'll have to do it while I'm on my honeymoon," Millie nodded at the bunk beds. "What will you do with all of this space after I move my stuff into Nic's apartment?"

"I plan to utilize every single inch of extra space," Danielle said. "Of course, you've been the perfect cabin mate, but having all of this space to myself will be sweet."

"Don't get too used to it," Millie warned. "I bet Donovan Sweeney is already plotting to move someone in here." Donovan was the ship's purser, in charge of all of the crew and staff, reporting only to Captain Armati.

"True." Danielle glanced at her watch. "I better shake my booty if I'm gonna make it upstairs in time for the morning torture session."

After Danielle left, Millie laid her wedding dress on her bunk bed and headed to the shower. Within a few short hours, she would be married, would be the captain's wife...Mrs. Millie Armati. It had a wonderful ring to it and Millie glanced at the sparkling diamond engagement ring on her finger.

She wondered if the crew and staff would treat her differently after Nic and she married. Millie hoped not. She would be the same Millie she'd always been.

Millie finished buttoning her blouse and slipped her lanyard over her head. If she hurried, she would have just enough time to grab a breakfast sandwich from the crew galley and eat it while she made her way upstairs.

She ran into Brody near the stairwell and they walked to the galley together.

"Today is your big day," Brody opened the door and held it while Millie stepped inside. "You look cool as a cucumber."

"Looks are deceiving, plus I have a full workload until two, so I don't have time to dwell on it," Millie said. "Are you going to be able to make it to the wedding?"

"I wouldn't miss it for the world," Brody said.

Nic and Millie had decided to have a small wedding ceremony, with family and a handful of their closest friends on board the ship. While the planned ceremony would be small, the reception would be a different story.

The couple wanted to make sure that all of the staff and crew were included. Instead of having a traditional wedding reception, it would be more of a wedding party open house that started right after the ceremony and continued into the evening. They hoped the flexible timeframe would give most, if not all, of the staff a chance to stop by and celebrate with them.

Annette was ready for the crowds and had prepared enough food to feed a small army. She'd even mapped out a spacious reception area on the lido deck, so that the ship's passengers would also be included in the celebration. There would be a champagne toast for the crew at six o'clock and then another for the ship's passengers at eight.

Staff Captain Vitale would be in charge of the ship until the wee hours of Monday morning when Captain Armati planned to take over and steer the ship into their honeymoon port of Philipsburg. If all of the preparation and planning went off without a hitch, it would be a miracle.

Millie darted from event to event and all along the way, the staff and crew stopped to wish her and the captain well. She took a brief break around one and managed to eat a cup of minestrone soup and a tossed salad. Millie was so nervous that she didn't dare eat anything else.

She finished the rest of her shift right on schedule, and then stopped by the cabin to grab her wedding dress and accessories. After a slight detour, she headed upstairs to the spa's changing room, where she planned to meet Annette, Cat and Danielle.

The trio was already there, dressed and impatiently waiting for the bride-to-be.

Annette jogged to the door and held it open while Millie carried her stuff inside. "We were getting ready to send out a search party."

"Sorry," Millie said breathlessly. "I got caught up with a customer complaint down at guest services." She paused to study Annette and Danielle, both wearing tea length, navy blue dresses they swore they would never wear. "You look gorgeous." She turned to Cat. "And of course, you, too."

"Especially Annette," Cat teased. "She cleans up nicely."

Annette grunted. "Yeah, well don't get used to it. As soon as the I-do's are over, I'm outta this getup. You shoulda heard the grief I got from Amit."

"I like it," Millie said. "Now all we need to do is to get you and Danielle dates."

"Danielle doesn't need a date," Cat said slyly. "Brody accompanied her up here. Talk about cleaning up nicely. He looks like he stepped off the pages of a GQ magazine."

Millie raised an eyebrow. "Danielle, is Brody your date?"

Danielle turned a tinge of pink. "I...we're just friends, but I have to admit he does look super-hot."

"What about Stephen Chow?" Danielle had recently gone on a date with Stephen Chow, the ship's acupuncturist.

"Not my type. Stephen was trying to turn me into a human pin cushion." She quickly changed the subject. "Let's get you dressed before Captain Armati starts thinking you left him at the altar."

Millie carried the dress to one of the large changing rooms, stepped inside and closed the door behind her. She hadn't tried on her wedding dress since the day she purchased it in Miami, convinced that if she did, she would jinx herself.

Her fingers trembled as she unzipped the garment bag and tugged the pale blue dress out of the bag. She slipped out of her uniform and eased the embellished drop waist dress over her head.

Millie ran her hand across the decorative beaded band circling her waist. She twisted to the side and eyed herself critically in the mirror. The dress sported a V-neck, but not too low. The cap sleeves were the perfect length and the hemline brushed the bottom of her knees.

Although the dress was a little loose, it wasn't enough to be noticeable and she decided it was perfect, giving her ample room to indulge in the delectable, decadent dishes Annette prepared for the wedding reception.

"Do you need help with the dress?" Cat hollered through the door.

"No. I'm almost ready." Millie deftly smoothed her hair back and secured it in a bun before pulling a few strands loose to frame her face. She reached into her tote bag, pulling out a small jewelry box and removing a heart-shaped diamond necklace from the box.

She remembered the moment Nic had surprised her with the necklace, telling her it was a promise...a promise of their future together. Millie rubbed the tip of her finger across the back and the initials "NDA," Niccolo Davide Armati.

"Beth and Bella are here," Annette announced.

"I'm almost ready." Millie adjusted the clasp of the necklace and stepped out of the changing room.

Danielle let out a wolf whistle. "Talk about cleaning up."

"Mom, you look beautiful," Beth gushed.

"Nana has a sparkly dress." Bella touched one of the beaded sleeves. "It's pretty."

"Thank you, Bella." Millie gently hugged her granddaughter. "You look very pretty, too. I love your dress."

"It's my favorite," Bella said solemnly.

"Are you ladies almost ready to go?" Beth asked. "Nic asked me to come down here to make sure you didn't have a sudden case of cold feet and jumped ship."

"Not at all. Not to mention it's too far to swim," Millie said. "Let me grab Nic's ring. It's here in my tote bag."

Millie reached into the bag, pulling out a second box containing Nic's wedding band, an embossed 14-karat two tone, white and gold band with a brushed finish. "I'm ready."

"It's time to get this wedding under way." Cat held the door and waited for the others to step into the hall. The women and Bella hurried down the corridor, passing several of the crew, who congratulated Millie and told her they planned to stop by later for the wedding celebration.

The Sky Chapel was one flight up and Millie held tight to the handrail as she ascended the steps.

By the time they reached the entrance to the chapel, she was feeling both lightheaded and nauseous. "I'm not sure if I want to throw up or pass out."

"You'll do neither." Beth grasped her mother's elbow in a firm grip. "It's just nerves. You'll be fine. Bella and I are heading inside." Beth kissed her mother's cheek before she and Bella slipped into the chapel.

Moments later, the faint echo of music began to play.

"That's our signal." Annette hugged Millie. "You got this," she whispered before she opened the door and stepped inside the crowded chapel.

Cat was next. "This is it. You're finally going to get your happily-ever-after." She gave Millie a quick hug and followed Annette inside.

Danielle peeked through the glass pane. "And...I'm up."

"Is Nic in there?" Millie swallowed nervously.

"Yes. He, along with Captain Vitale, Andy and First Officer Craig McMasters," Danielle said. "Now all they're waiting for is you."

She turned to Millie, noting her friend's pale, pasty complexion. "My brother, Casey, used to tell me, 'In the end, our only regrets are the chances we didn't take, the relationships we were afraid to have, and the decisions we waited too long to make.' I love you like a mother."

"And I love you like one of my own, Danielle," Millie gave her young friend a watery smile. "Now get going before I freak out or start bawling."

Danielle handed Millie the bouquet of flowers and slipped inside the chapel, leaving Millie all alone.

She could hear the music and the murmur of voices, and she closed her eyes. "Dear Lord. Thank you for bringing Nic into my life. Please bless our marriage and let us have many happy years together," she whispered.

Millie grasped the door handle and pulled it open. The pianist began playing the wedding march as Millie began to make her way to the front of the chapel.

She fixed her gaze on Nic and their eyes locked. At that moment, the tension started to leave Millie's body and she relaxed her grip on the flowers. It was going to be all right. In fact, it was going to be better than all right. Millie was marrying the man of her dreams.

Her gaze never wavered as she continued her slow walk to the man who would be her husband. When she reached the front, Nic squeezed her hand. "I love you," he whispered.

"I love you too."

"Then let's get you two hitched," Pastor Evans quipped and the guests chuckled.

The ceremony was brief and in the blink of an eye, he pronounced Millie and Nic husband and wife.

Nic swept Millie into his arms and kissed his bride...a deep, passionate kiss that took Millie's breath away.

"Get a room," Brody teased.

"Oh, we will," Nic shot back and winked at his head of night security. Millie turned to hug Annette, whose eyes were suspiciously red.

Cat didn't even attempt to keep her tears in check as they streamed down her cheeks.

Danielle wrapped her arms around Millie. "You were the most beautiful bride and I'm sure gonna miss having you around."

Millie tightened her grip. "I'm not going anywhere," she promised her young friend.

Nic and Millie switched sides and Millie hugged Captain Vitale…Antonio, Andy and First Officer McMasters. The couple led the way out of the chapel and waited for the guests to make their way out.

Millie hugged her family, her friends and her co-workers. There was one person notably absent, Nic's daughter, Fiona. She started to comment, but stopped herself, sad that Fiona couldn't - wouldn't - be there, but vowing to accept the situation as it was and continue to pray there would be healing in Fiona's heart.

The ship's main theater set the stage for the large reception. Navy blue streamers streamed from the ceiling and clusters of silver and gold helium balloons decorated the tables.

After a first toast, the couple loaded their plates with delectable dishes Annette, Amit and the kitchen staff had prepared. There was an array of tempting treats, from the wrapped bacon mac and cheese bites to large pots of Italian meatballs, finger sandwiches and a variety of side dishes. There were also several antipasto platters and a decadent array of desserts.

The couple had just finished their food when a commotion near the exit doors caught their attention. Oscar, one of the head security officers, stood blocking the entrance and shaking his head.

Alarmed, Millie shoved her chair back. "I wonder what's going on."

Nic leaned to the left. "It's one of the ship's crewmembers. He works down in maintenance. I think his name is Sherman something, but he goes by another nickname."

"Sharky," Millie said.

"That's it." Nic shot his wife a quick glance. "You know him?"

Oscar stepped to the side and the room grew quiet as Sharky aka Sherman Kiveski, steered a handcart, sporting a large, bulky item strapped to the front, into the reception area.

Millie's eyes widened. "What in the world is that?"

Chapter 6

"It looks like a shark," Nic whispered.

Sharky caught Millie's eye and picked up the pace as he pushed the handcart and the metal shark to the table. "I gotcha a wedding gift, but I don't see a gift table."

"Captain." Sharky saluted Nic and smiled at Millie. "I tried wrapping it, but the paper kept ripping on the fins."

"I..." Millie slowly stood, staring at the pointed metal teeth of the shark. "I don't know what to say."

Nic joined her and they made their way around the table. "This is the most original wedding gift I've ever laid eyes on."

Sharky proudly patted the shark's snout. "This here is a one of a kind. I've been workin' on this baby ever since I heard about the engagement. I nicknamed him Finley, but you can pick whatever name you want."

Felippe, one of the security guards, made his way over. "I can take this up to your apartment captain."

"Thanks, Felippe, I would appreciate it."

"After I drop it off, I'll return the handcart to maintenance." Felippe reached for the handle of the handcart.

Sharky tightened his grip on the handle. "You gotta handle it with kid gloves. If you're not careful, Finley's fins will get caught in the doorway and they'll bend."

"I'll be careful Sharky." Felippe jerked the handcart from Sharky's grasp, nodded at the captain and wheeled the shiny sea creature out of the room.

Sharky turned his attention to Millie. "Haven't seen you around the maintenance area lately. Things must be quiet up here."

"I've been busy with work and the wedding," Millie mumbled.

"I bet." Sharky rubbed his hands together. "Rumor has it there's some good grub in here."

"The buffet is over there." Millie pointed to the tables of food. "I'm sorry to say there's no hot sauce."

"No worries. I still got a little left from before. I'm sure I'll find something to fill my belly." Sharky patted his protruding stomach. "Woo-hoo." He squinted his eyes. "Is that Annette over there, wearing a dress? She is one sexy mama in that outfit."

Sharky made a beeline for Annette, who stood near the buffet table, talking to one of the kitchen staff.

"Isn't he married?" Nic asked.

"I believe so," Millie replied. "As surprising as that may be."

Nic turned to his bride. "You frequent the maintenance area?"

"I've been down there once or twice. Sharky and Reef, the night maintenance supervisor, have helped out with a couple of recent investigations."

"Ah," Nic said. "Now I remember. The last one involved Ted Danvers' girlfriend. What was her name?"

"Brigitte."

"What have I gotten myself into?" Nic snaked an arm around his wife's waist and pulled her close.

"Nothing you can't handle," Millie said.

The rest of the afternoon and evening was a whirlwind of happy moments, first dances, a bouquet toss and even a cupcake-cutting event. One of Millie's favorite gifts was a four-foot tall, handmade wedding card, signed by all of the crew and staff.

After the first part of the day's festivities wrapped up, the couple and wedding party moved to the lido deck to celebrate with the ship's guests. It was one of the happiest days of Millie's life, and she tried to take it all in, to tuck it away in her memory to save forever.

All the while, a glimmer of hope that Fiona would make an appearance lingered in the back of her mind, but she never showed. Finally, it was time to turn in and Millie's stomach did a small flip when Nic leaned close and whispered in her ear. "Are you ready to head home?"

"Yes." Millie sucked in a breath. "I've been looking forward to and dreading this moment since you proposed."

"Don't worry. I don't bite. Maybe nibble on you a little," he teased.

Millie met her husband's gaze. "I'll hold you to that."

***

Nic and Millie were up early the next morning, with Nic making his way to the bridge before the first glimmer of daylight, to assist Captain Vitale in steering the ship into Philipsburg's port.

While Nic headed to the bridge, Millie packed their bags for the weeklong honeymoon. Captain Vitale, who would be filling in for Nic during their absence, graciously offered to stay in the apartment to care for Scout.

It would work out perfectly. The only cloud on the horizon Millie could see was Fiona had never shown up for the wedding or the reception, and Millie still hadn't met her new stepdaughter.

Nic tried to assure his wife that Fiona would eventually come to terms with their marriage, but Millie wasn't convinced. She had no idea what to expect, and began fearing the worst.

After she finished packing, Millie slid the balcony door open and stepped onto the deck, balancing her cup of coffee on top of the railing. She leaned forward and craned her neck in an attempt to catch her first glimpse of their honeymoon destination.

The ship had reached the bay and already started to make the turn to begin the daunting task of docking the mega cruise ship. It slowed to a crawl and began to shudder as it inched its way toward the pier.

Millie was always fascinated at how Nic and the other captains were able to maneuver the massive cruise ship into a small space making it look easy, all the while managing to avoid a collision with the docking area.

The crew on the dock grabbed the ropes and began securing the ship.

Scout followed Millie out onto the balcony and she reached down to scoop him up in her free arm. "Would you like to go for a walk?"

Scout let out a low whine, which Millie took for a 'yes.' She downed the last of her coffee and set the cup in the kitchen sink before exiting the apartment.

They stopped to see Andy first, and then swung by Millie's old cabin to say good-bye to Danielle.

The cabin was empty, so Millie and Scout headed upstairs to thank Cat and Annette for all of their help.

Annette was prepping for the afternoon tea and she stopped working when Millie walked in. "You look like you're raring to go."

"I am," Millie said. "I wanted to thank you for preparing such a spectacular wedding feast. Everything was delicious."

"You're welcome. It was a beautiful wedding."

"It was." Millie crossed her arms. "I saw you dancing with Sharky."

"Good heavens." Annette rolled her eyes. "That man would not leave me alone. He followed me around half the night. I told him if I danced with him once, he had to promise he would buzz off."

"You did?"

"Yeah, and he told me to keep up with the sweet nothings because it was turning him on."

Millie laughed. "Oh dear. Poor Sharky."

"Poor Sharky?" Annette gasped. "What about poor Annette?"

"You can handle Sharky." Millie glanced at her watch. "I better get going. I want to stop by to thank Cat before I head back to the cabin to meet Nic and grab our stuff."

Annette walked Millie to the galley door. "Have you heard anything else about those dead people at the resort where you'll be honeymooning?"

Millie frowned. She'd completely forgotten about the deaths at the Grand Bay Beach Club. "No. I forgot. Hopefully, the police have cleared Regan."

Annette pushed the swinging door open and followed Millie into the corridor. "I'm sure you'll have a great time. Don't worry about us. We'll hold down the fort, or in this case, the ship. Enjoy your time off."

Millie gave Annette a quick hug, thanking her again for all of her hard work and then headed to the gift shop. Although Ocean Treasures was closed while the ship was in port, she caught a glimpse of Cat in the back and lightly tapped on the glass.

Cat gave a quick nod and hurried to the door. "I wondered if you were going to have time to stop by before you got off the ship."

"I wanted to thank you for all you did, for your moral support and for being a great friend."

"You're welcome. I loved every minute of it," Cat said. "Did you see Annette and Sharky dancing?"

"Yeah. Annette said he kept bugging her, so she finally agreed to one dance. I thought he was married."

"Nah." Cat waved dismissively. "He likes to tell people he is, but he's not. He sure seems smitten with Annette. I ran into Malene, who manages the flower shop and she told me Sharky stopped by there first thing this morning and ordered a bouquet of flowers to be delivered to the galley."

"Oh dear." Millie grinned. "I wish I could be there to see the look on Annette's face when the flowers show up."

"I may not be there to see her reaction, but I bet I'll be able to hear it from here," Cat said. "And did you happen to see Danielle and Brody at the reception? They were so cute together."

Millie had noticed. She'd never pictured Brody and Danielle together, but after seeing them, she decided they made a perfect couple. Brody was sensible, strong, quiet and steady while Danielle could be more impulsive, headstrong and, in Millie's opinion, reckless. "Yes, I was surprised, but in a good way."

The store phone began ringing.

"I better head out. Thanks again, Cat, and I'll see you next week."

"Have fun! We'll miss you."

Millie exited the store and started down the stairs to her cabin when she remembered it wasn't her cabin anymore. She made her way to the lido deck to search for Danielle one last time before searching the main areas of the ship.

Her radio was in the apartment, on the charger since she was officially "off-duty," so she made another trip to her former cabin where she let herself inside and jotted a quick note to Danielle, thanking her for everything. She also told her she would miss her and warned her to behave herself while she was gone.

When she reached the apartment, her new home, she double-checked to make sure she had everything and had just finished when Nic made his way inside.

Millie's heart fluttered at the sight of her handsome husband.

"Are you ready to go?" he asked.

"I am. Scout and I made our rounds, saying goodbye to Andy, Cat and Annette. I couldn't find Danielle, so I left her a note and told her to stay out of trouble."

Nic pulled his wife into his arms and Millie melted under the steamy kiss as she remembered the night before. The tips of her ears burned at the memory and finally, she pulled back. "Keep it up and we'll never leave the apartment."

"Is that such a bad thing?" Nic reluctantly released his grip and pushed the large suitcase toward the door while Millie scooped Scout up and held him close. "You better behave too," she said as she nuzzled him.

"He'll surely keep Antonio on his toes." Nic patted his pooch and scratched under his chin before Millie set him on the floor.

"Let's get this honeymoon underway." Millie maneuvered her small carry-on bag out of the apartment.

The couple stopped briefly in the bridge while Nic gave Captain Vitale and First Officer McMasters a few final instructions and checked to make sure they had his personal cell phone number to call in the event of an emergency.

Beth had left a voice mail on her mother's phone, letting her know they were already off the ship and planned to do some sightseeing on the island before meeting up with them later.

Millie secretly suspected Beth intentionally made plans, so that Nic and Millie could settle into their hotel room and have some alone time. "Have you talked with Fiona?" she asked after they climbed into the taxi.

"She's already at the resort," Nic said. "I think she'll see us later, for dinner. I called Regan earlier and told him we would be arriving around eleven. I haven't seen Regan in a couple of years."

Nic had told his wife that Regan and he had grown up together in the small village of Bertoli, gone to grade school together and even college. They lost touch for a while, but reconnected when he joined Majestic Cruise Lines and discovered his friend owned a swanky resort on the shores of Saint-Martin.

"Have you heard anything else about the unfortunate deaths at the resort?" Millie asked.

"No." Nic shook his head. "Our conversation was brief."

Millie stared out the window as the taxi wound its way around the island, crossing over from Sint Maarten, the Dutch side of the island, to Saint-Martin, the French side. If she hadn't caught a glimpse of the bright green and white sign that read, *Bienvenue en Partie Francaise, Welcome to the French Side,* she never would've known they were in another country.

It took another fifteen minutes to reach the sprawling resort. Millie craned her neck and caught a glimpse of the turquoise waters as the taxi made its way to the resort's main entrance.

Nic helped Millie out of the taxi and then joined the driver in unloading their luggage from the trunk.

After paying, the couple stepped inside the large lobby with soaring ceilings. A center fountain bubbled and Millie stepped closer to inspect it.

"I think I have a penny or two, if you'd like to make a wish." Nic fished some coins out of his pocket and handed one to Millie.

"I have everything I could ever want or need," Millie said. "But a million bucks wouldn't hurt either." She tossed the coin into the pool and waited while her husband did the same. "What was your wish?"

"Haven't you ever heard that it's bad luck to tell your wishes?" Nic teased.

"I told you mine." Millie followed her husband around the side of the fountain to the check-in line.

"Which is why we probably won't see those million dollars."

The uniformed woman at the counter motioned them forward. "Checking in?"

"Yes. Niccolo and Millie Armati."

The woman smiled broadly. "Mr. Leclerc has been eagerly awaiting your arrival. One moment." She held up a finger and picked up the telephone handset. "Yes. Mr. Leclerc. The Armatis are here, checking in."

"It has such a nice ring to it. Millie Armati," Millie whispered in her husband's ear.

"I agree," Nic said.

"I will." The woman replaced the handset. "Regan…Mr. Leclerc is on his way."

"Nic." A man's booming voice echoed across the lobby and Millie turned to watch a tall man with white hair stroll towards them. "It's good to see you, my friend." He grasped Nic's hand, shook it violently and slapped him on the shoulder before turning his attention to Millie. "This is your beautiful bride?"

"Yes, this is Millie."

Regan shook Millie's hand so hard her head began to wobble. Finally, he released his grip. "Congratulations. Welcome to Grand Bay Beach Club. You're staying in one of the seaside cottages. It's a little more private than the hotel, although you're only steps away from the restaurants, bars, pools, nightclubs, not to mention the beach."

Regan motioned to a man standing near the entrance and he made his way over. "Dennis. Can you make sure this luggage is delivered to Castaway Cottage? Dennis is in charge of the porters. He can help in whatever way necessary."

Dennis reached for the luggage handle. "It's a pleasure to meet you. Regan talks very highly of you."

"I can take care of my small suitcase and purse," Millie said.

Dennis nodded. "As you wish."

Nic waited until Dennis departed with their suitcase. "Has there been anything new to report on the deaths of the two people here at the resort?"

Regan's smile faded. "There's been no new news on the investigation. Unfortunately, there's been another death. A guest found one of our groundskeepers floating face down in a koi pond early this morning."

Chapter 7

"The groundskeeper's name was George," Regan said. "He's worked here forever. When I bought the resort years ago, he came with it. He's been around longer than I have." Regan lowered his voice. "The situation is becoming direr by the minute. The authorities were here again this morning questioning me. There's no rhyme or reason to the deaths."

He went on to explain that Raoul, one of the resort's desk clerks, was found inside the walk-in freezer in the kitchen. "At first, we believed it was an isolated incident and he somehow managed to accidentally become trapped inside, but after the second death, a female guest a couple of days later, we began to suspect something more sinister was afoot. With the discovery of George's body, we're certain of it."

"Is there any connection between the three people who died?" Millie had promised herself she wouldn't become involved, but the mystery was hard to resist.

"Not that I'm aware of," Regan shook his head. "The only common thread is all three died here, and all within the last week. George left an urgent message on my cell phone, asking if he could talk to me first thing this morning."

Millie's mind whirled. "Maybe he was onto the killer."

"I suspect that may be the case." Regan gazed over Millie's head. "Ah. There's my wife, Nadia."

A slender woman with light brown skin hurried across the lobby floor. Her sharp, dark eyes flitted from her husband to Nic. The woman reached for Nic's hand. "Nic, it's so nice to see you again."

She turned to Millie. "You must be Millie." She grasped Millie's hand in a firm grip and smiled warmly. "It's a pleasure to finally meet you."

Nadia turned to Nic. "Regan has been chomping at the bit, waiting for your arrival. I'm only sorry you've come at a time where we find ourselves under a slight duress."

"We heard," Millie folded her arms. "And I'm so sorry. What terrible tragedies."

"Very much so. George was like family to us." Nadia turned to her husband. "I'm sure you would like to catch up with Nic and since he's already been here before and is familiar with the grounds, I can take Millie on a tour, show her all the resort has to offer."

"Splendid idea dear," Regan nodded. "If you don't mind?"

"Not at all," Millie said. "Nic and I have a whole week together."

"Perfect." Nadia placed a light hand on Millie's arm. "We can start in the lounge area."

"Now don't you go dragging Millie into our mess." Regan wagged his finger at his wife and she batted her eyes innocently. "I have no idea what you're talking about."

"The deaths," Regan said bluntly. "I knew I never should've mentioned to Nadia that your wife has a knack for solving mysteries."

"She does," Nic shook his head. "I can already see the look in her eyes."

"As I see in Nadia's," Regan said.

"You have nothing to worry about," Nadia insisted. "We're just going to tour the resort."

Nic gave his wife a quick kiss. "Double the trouble."

Millie followed Nadia through the lobby and down a long hall, where she abruptly stopped. "Did you hear that?"

"Hear what?"

"Footsteps," Nadia whispered. "Like someone is following us."

"No." Millie shook her head. "I didn't hear anything."

Nadia began walking again, this time at a slower pace.

The hall opened into another large area, this one an octagon shape. Floor-to-ceiling windows lined the walls. "We have a gym over here. There's an indoor / outdoor pool directly across from the gym. We also have a conference center, a snack bar and a game room."

"This is overwhelming." Millie slowly turned in a circle. "It would take more than a week to do everything."

"We also have a sports stand near the beach where guests can rent kayaks, paddleboards, paddleboats and snorkel gear. All guests have access to beach chairs and beach umbrellas. We even offer bar service, delivered right to your lounge chair."

Nadia and Millie continued their tour of the grounds and finished near a crescent shaped sandy white beach. Off to the side and tucked behind lush tropical greenery were several beach cottages.

"You're staying in my favorite cottage. We call it Castaway Cottage. It's more secluded than the others and surrounded on three sides by palm trees and greenery. We carved out a clearing and there's a spectacular view of the ocean from the front porch rocking chairs."

"It's beautiful," Millie murmured. "I can't believe we'll be staying here for a week."

"The place is clean. I checked it myself, so you won't have to worry about anyone listening in on your conversations."

"Someone is going to listen in on my conversations?" Millie asked.

"I can't prove it, but I think someone, maybe the killer, has strategically planted listening devices around the resort," Nadia led Millie to the cottage on the end and they stepped onto the porch.

"Poor George's body was found less than thirty feet from here. I still can't believe it."

She swiped her card across the magnetic door strip and pushed the door open. "Regan keeps telling me to let the authorities handle the investigations, but I feel like we're sitting ducks, waiting for the next murder."

"What do you think is going on?" Millie asked.

"I've been going crazy, trying to figure out who might have it in for Regan and me and why now?" Nadia stepped inside the cottage, held a finger to her lips and tilted her head. "Coast is clear."

"I hope so." Millie followed her inside and then paused to take it all in. "This is perfect. I love it."

The cottage was cheery, brightened by the whitewashed walls. The front door opened to a living room area where a comfy plush sofa and matching loveseat faced a small brick fireplace.

To the left of the living room was a table, large enough to seat six. Beyond that was a spacious, state-of-the-art kitchen.

"The bedroom and bath are over here." Nadia led her to an antique barn door and slid it open before stepping to the side. "There's a king-size bed, so you should have plenty of room. There's only one bath, but it has a connecting door in the master suite and another one that leads into the hallway."

Millie stepped over to the window and tilted the plantation shutters as she peeked out. There was a partial view of the ocean. "I don't know how Nic and I will ever be able to repay you for your generosity and hospitality."

"I do," Nadia smiled. "We're coming on a cruise later this year, after the summer rush is over and before the holiday crowds arrive."

"We'll be sure to find you the perfect suite," Millie promised. The women stepped back into the living room.

"I think Regan is going to bring Nic over here after they catch up." Nadia walked into the kitchen and opened the refrigerator door. "There's a tray of goodies in here in case you're hungry. I also made a batch of my special island concoction. I call it the breezy beachcomber."

She lifted a glass pitcher from the fridge and set it on the counter. "The drink is an equal mix of orange, pineapple and passion fruit, with a splash of ginger ale and lemonade." Nadia filled two glasses and handed one to Millie.

"Thank you." Millie sipped the fruity concoction. "This is delicious. I should get the recipe for Annette. She manages our food and beverage department."

Nadia set her glass on the counter and hopped onto an empty barstool. "So tell me all about yourself. Regan almost fell out of his chair when he heard Nic was getting married. He was devastated after Lisa's death and Fiona took her mother's death extremely hard. What do you think of Fiona?"

"She didn't show up for the dinner Saturday evening where we planned to meet and then she never showed up for the wedding." Millie told Nadia that, at first, Fiona told her father she was suffering from jet lag. "But when she didn't show up for the wedding, I knew there was more to the story."

"Oh dear." Nadia rubbed her forehead. "I'm sorry to hear that. You still haven't met?"

"No." Millie shook her head. "Nic said she plans to meet us for dinner this evening, but I'm not holding my breath. Have you met Fiona?"

"Yes. It was several years ago. Nic brought Lisa and Fiona here for a few days," Nadia said.

"What was Lisa like?"

"She was a sweet woman. Lisa had a gentle personality. She was quiet, more of an introvert I would say. She loved to cook and even helped prepare a special French meal for her family while she was here."

"So the complete opposite of me," Millie grimaced.

"There's nothing wrong with that," Nadia said. "She definitely would not have enjoyed being in the spotlight, in a job say, for example, as an assistant cruise director. I, on the other hand, think it would be a dream job."

Millie told Nadia she loved her job, loved meeting new people and traveling to new places. "God put me in the right place at the right time. After my husband, Roger, left, I thought my life was over, but it was simply the end of one chapter and the beginning of another."

Millie sipped her drink, thinking of how blessed she was and how much she loved her husband. "I hate to keep pumping you for information, but what do you think of Fiona."

Nadia studied Millie for a moment and Millie could see she was mulling over her answer, carefully choosing her words. "She loves her father very much and Fiona and Lisa were close. Of course, Nic was at sea for months at a time, so it was just the two women. She was an only child and a little..." Nadia's voice trailed off as she searched for the right word.

"Indulged?" Millie prompted.

"Yes." Nadia nodded. "Indulged."

"Great," Millie groaned. "She's going to hate me forever."

"I'm not so sure about that. I think you're the perfect match for Nic. You're funny. You're full of spunk. You love adventure."

"And a good mystery, which has gotten me into more hot water than I care to admit."

"I heard all about it," Nadia chuckled. "Speaking of mystery, I have to figure out what's going on here at Grand Bay. Poor Raoul. He was the first one to die and what an awful death, to be trapped inside a freezer and freeze to death."

Millie's stomach churned at the thought. "I'm sure I would've passed out from my claustrophobia before I froze. Remind me again, who Raoul was."

"He was one of our desk clerks. Raoul worked the night shift with another of the male clerks," Nadia said. "We schedule the men to work during the night, leaving the day shift for the female employees for safety reasons, although now it seems kind of ironic."

"Did Raoul have any known enemies; have any recent arguments with a co-worker, anything that might be a clue?" Millie asked.

Nadia bit her upper lip and gazed at Millie thoughtfully. "No. As far as I know, he was well liked by all of his co-workers. He has been, I mean, was with us for over a year."

"What about the woman...the guest?" Millie prompted.

"Ellen Fulbright. She and her husband arrived here three days before her death. They were a fun couple, a little younger, maybe in their mid-forties. The last time I saw them was the other night when they were in the lounge listening to karaoke."

"Did Ellen and her husband..." Millie's voice trailed off.

"Gordy. Ellen and Gordy Fulbright. They were from Kansas City, somewhere in the states."

"Did Ellen and Gordy get along, as far as you could tell?"

"I didn't know them well, but they seemed to get along." Nadia placed both hands in her lap and gazed at Millie earnestly. "Don't tell Regan, but I've been doing a little digging around myself and there are no red flags, nothing that appears to connect the deaths."

"The only link is your resort." Millie drummed her fingers on the countertop. "Motive and opportunity. This is a large resort, with hundreds of guests coming and going on a daily basis, not to mention dozens of employees. The guest, Ellen, would have had to let someone into her room."

"Unless they had a master key," Nadia said.

"True." Millie began to pace. "Possibly someone with a good bit of knowledge about the resort, to not only gain access to a guest's room, but also have access to the kitchen and walk-in freezer."

"Not necessarily," Nadia shifted uneasily. "We offer free tours of the kitchen and the grounds on a regular basis, and one of our chefs hosts a French cooking class for our guests. It's held in the kitchen, which means any number of our guests would be familiar with the layout."

"There goes that theory. I suppose someone could've tricked Ellen into unlocking the hotel room door, perhaps telling her they were from the housekeeping department." Millie stopped pacing. "What about surveillance cameras in the hall?"

"We, along with the authorities, have already looked at them. Ellen entered her room at 9:00

a.m. She was wearing workout clothes and we tracked her on another video in the workout room with Gordy." Nadia went on to explain Gordy had an airtight alibi. He stayed in the workout room before hitting the sauna. His room card wasn't used again until 11:30 a.m., when he returned to their room and found Ellen in the tub.

"So we're back to square one," Millie said.

"In a nutshell." Nadia tugged on a stray strand of hair. "I do have at least one person I think might be trying to set Regan and me up."

Millie interrupted. "Let me get a pad of paper and pen." She snatched her purse off the counter and pulled out a pen and small notepad. "I'm ready."

"It's Wayne Clemson. If I had to put my money on anyone, it would be Wayne. He's Regan's former business partner and the two are embroiled in a nasty lawsuit."

Millie perked up. "What kind of lawsuit?"

"Regan caught Wayne skimming money off the top, that and he was handling the books and not paying taxes."

"He sounds like a shyster." Millie carefully printed his name in her notepad.

Nadia wiped the condensation off the bottom of her glass. "He's a creep."

Millie studied the name. "It's a start. Too bad I can't take a look at the crime scenes."

"I thought you'd never ask." Nadia hopped off the barstool. "We can, but we better go now, before the men show up."

Millie downed the last of her fruity concoction and set the empty drink glass in the sink. "Lead the way."

Chapter 8

Nadia jotted a note for her husband and Nic, and left it on the cottage counter. "Let's head to the koi pond and gardens first. It's where George's body was found this morning."

The women walked along the sandy beach before turning onto a paved path not far from the cottage. A strong woodsy smell with a hint of garlic permeated the heavy humid air.

"What's that smell?" Millie asked.

"Lantana." Nadia pointed at an array of pink and orange flowers lining the path. "It's our national flower. The butterflies love them." As if to prove the point, a monarch butterfly flitted over Millie's head and landed on a nearby bud.

"That's cool." The soothing sound of tinkling water grew louder as they continued to meander down the curved walkway. They rounded a bend and Millie spotted a pond where a school of orange fish congregated under an arched bridge.

"Shh. Do you hear that?" Nadia parted a cluster of bushes and peered inside. "I could've sworn I heard someone cough."

Millie shook her head. "I didn't hear anything."

"Huh." Nadia released her grip on the bush and it snapped back in place. "A hotel guest found George right about here." She pointed to the water. "The authorities already removed the yellow tape."

Millie stepped to the edge of the pond and studied the pool of water. "What time this morning?"

"Before ten, at least that's what time the guest reported finding the body," Nadia said.

"Is this a lighted path, where guests might come this way in the evening or at all hours?"

"Yes. It's one of several paths leading to the beach," Nadia said. "All of our paths are well-lit for liability purposes."

Millie circled the pond. She pulled her cell phone from her purse and snapped several pictures. "Where to next?"

"Let's head to the walk-in freezer. The authorities and health inspectors finally gave us the okay to start using it again. Of course, they wanted to inspect it to make sure it was functioning properly."

Millie opened her mouth to ask if the freezer passed the inspection, but Nadia beat her to it.

"It passed with flying colors. We had it serviced six months ago, so Raoul wasn't trapped by accident. Someone locked him in there."

"I think I would rather drown," Millie groaned.

"Me too." The women rounded the side of the building. "We'll go in through the back."

Millie followed Nadia into the large, open kitchen. The smell of French fries and baked bread filled the air and Millie's stomach growled. "I guess I should've munched on some goodies while we were at the cottage."

"Have a piece of fruit." Nadia snatched a bunch of bananas off the counter and handed one to Millie.

"Thanks." Millie peeled the banana and took a big bite. "So where's the freezer?"

"Over here." Nadia wound her way around the gleaming stainless steel counters, past a large butcher block cutting board and stopped in front of a massive metal door. She flipped the handle and pulled the door open.

Millie eased past Nadia and peered into the cold, dark space. "Is there a light?"

Nadia fumbled for the switch and bright light illuminated the interior.

"What a terrible place to die." Millie took a tentative step inside the freezer and studied the large, metal shelves that lined the walls. They were filled with packets of meat.

"We got a large shipment of goods today. We also freeze some of our fresh fruits and vegetables when they're in season." Nadia pointed to a section of terra-cotta floor tiles near the door. "This is where one of our kitchen workers found Raoul. There are scratch marks on the door and the frame where he tried to pry the door open, trying to escape."

Millie gazed at the rest of her uneaten banana. "I'm not hungry anymore."

"I don't blame you." The women stepped back into the kitchen, and Nadia shut off the freezer light and closed the door. "It's hard to erase the image from my mind."

Nadia pointed at the banana. "You sure you're up to seeing the guest room where Ellen was found?"

"Yes." Millie forced herself to finish the food and tossed the banana peel in the garbage can on the way out.

"It's a bit of a hike. I hope you don't mind walking."

"Not at all," Millie said.

The women walked for what Millie guessed was about ten minutes before Nadia stopped abruptly in front of a sprawling, multistoried building. "This is it." She motioned Millie to a bank of elevators.

"I don't do elevators," Millie said as she fell into step.

"You weren't kidding about the claustrophobia." Nadia nodded her head. "The stairs are over there. The room is on the second floor."

"I like stairs," Millie said. "I'll meet you up there."

"Okie dokie." Nadia punched the *up* button and Millie darted into the stairwell. When Millie emerged, Nadia was standing in the hall waiting for her.

"Are you sure you climbed the stairs? You're not even out of breath."

"I've had a lot of practice. I don't take elevators unless absolutely necessary or I'm unconscious," Millie said.

"Duly noted." Nadia grinned. "The guest room is down here."

The women marched to the end of the corridor, to the very last room on the right and Millie stood off to the side while Nadia slipped a keycard in the slot above the door handle.

"Are there surveillance cameras on this floor?" Millie asked.

"Down there, close to the elevators."

Millie narrowed her eyes and gazed at the area they'd just left. She shifted her gaze to the door directly across the hall from the room. "Is that another guest room?"

"No, it's a housekeeping closet." Nadia swung the door open and Millie followed her into the room. "Since sleuthing is your field of expertise, I need some pointers on what to look for."

"First, I try to put myself in the killer's shoes. The last thing you want is to get caught, so you're looking for the easiest, quickest way to access your victim, if you will." Millie wandered past the bathroom, and into the main part of the guest room.

The room was tidy, the beds made. There was a placard propped up next to the flat screen television, welcoming the new guest. "Housekeeping has already cleaned?"

"Yes," Nadia nodded. "Regan was anxious to get the room cleaned and back to business as usual. He didn't want to scare the guests, although a few of them questioned housekeeping when we first called the police and crime scene investigators showed up."

"I see." Millie walked to the set of sliders, flipped the latch and stepped onto the balcony. Nadia followed her out.

Millie leaned over the side of the railing and studied the meticulously manicured grounds. "It would be easy for someone to reach this second floor balcony." She pointed to the corner of the building. "There are tall shrubs all the way to the corner. Someone could easily creep along the side of the building, climb to the second story and vault over the side of this low railing without being seen."

"The slider would have to be unlocked for them to get inside," Nadia pointed out.

"True." Millie stepped inside and knelt down to inspect the slider's lock. "This is a flip lever lock. I had one of these in my house in Michigan and swapped it out after my son showed me how easy it was to get inside." She stood. "Come inside and lock the door."

The women traded places. Nadia slid the slider shut and flipped the lock latch before giving Millie a thumbs up.

Millie grasped the center of the sliding glass door pull and gave it several quick jerks, causing the inside lever to move. Within moments, Millie slid the slider open.

Nadia's mouth fell open. "Oh my gosh. It took you like five seconds to open the locked slider."

"Yep. Scary, huh?"

"We need to get all of the slider locks changed out," Nadia said. "I had no idea."

"Most people wouldn't, unless you're a criminal. It might not be as important on the upper floors, but these lower floors? I would definitely change them out on the lower floors and install an extra safety mechanism on the inside."

Millie stepped inside and flipped the lever. "I wouldn't mind taking a look at the bathtub, where the guest's body was found."

The guest bathroom was spacious, larger than Millie envisioned. There was a granite counter with double sinks, a separate shower and spa tub. "This is lovely."

"Thanks." Nadia smiled. "We're remodeling all of the bathrooms in this building. We've already finished both the first and second floors and recently started on the third floor."

Millie tiptoed to the other side of the bathroom and focused her attention on the spa tub. "You could almost fit two people in this."

"Yes. There's an identical one in your cottage. You and your new husband should check it out," Nadia teased.

The tips of Millie's ears started to burn and she smiled. "We might have to do that." Her eyes slowly scanned the room, but nothing inside the bathroom hit her sleuthing radar. "I haven't seen anything that appears to be a clue, other than the fact the slider could have easily been jimmied open and the shrubs outside make a perfect cover."

Millie shifted to the side. "I'm sure the authorities have a file full of pictures of the crime scenes."

"They're not the only one," Nadia said.

Millie lifted a brow. "You have pictures?"

"I don't have a file full, but I did take a few pictures of this room before the authorities arrived. I wasn't around when Raoul's body was discovered. Regan was out playing golf the morning Ellen's body was found." Nadia wrinkled her nose. "Regan was furious I took photos, but after Raoul's death, I began to suspect there was something more going on."

"Where are the pictures now?" Millie asked.

"On my phone." Nadia pulled her cell phone from her pocket, switched it on and scrolled through the screen before handing it to Millie. "A couple of the photos are kind of blurry since I had to hurry and Gordy was nearby, calling Ellen's family."

Millie fumbled in her purse and pulled out her reading glasses before slipping them on. She noted the position of the woman's body, how one hand covered her mouth while the other rested near her head.

"See how she has two fingers pointing up?" Nadia shivered. "I had no idea what it meant until we found George's body in the koi pond. Do you think the killer plans on killing again?"

That would be Millie's guess, but she didn't want to alarm her new friend. "I hope not," she said. "Wait a minute..." Millie tapped the screen to enlarge the picture, focusing her attention on the woman's right hand. "We can rule out robbery for this one."

"We can?" Nadia peered over Millie's shoulder.

"See the large diamond ring on Ellen's right hand? If this was a robbery, the killer would have taken the diamond ring." Millie lifted her gaze. "Do you know if anything else was taken from the room? Wallet, cash, credit cards?"

"No." Nadia shook her head. "It looked like someone had ransacked the place, but I don't recall Gordy mentioning anything being stolen. Of course, the authorities aren't telling us anything yet since technically, Regan and I are both suspects."

Millie handed the phone to Nadia. "The killer took the time to place Ellen's body in the tub and even position the body in a specific pose. The room had been ransacked." She tapped her toe on the floor. "Whoever it was went through the couple's belongings, but as far as you know, nothing was stolen."

"Unless Gordy is hiding something," Nadia said. "The authorities did tell him he couldn't leave the island yet. He didn't want to stay here, so he checked out yesterday. I'm not sure where he went."

"The killer took his time here, which means he - or she - wasn't concerned they would be caught," Millie said.

"You think Ellen's husband, Gordy, killed his wife?" Nadia asked.

"It's still too early to tell, but I'm moving him to the top of the list of suspects."

Chapter 9

The women returned to the cottage at the same time Nic and Regan arrived.

While Nadia poured more of her fruity concoction, Millie pulled the snack tray from the fridge, added some crackers to the side and carried the tray to the table. She swayed slightly as she eased the tray onto the table.

"Are you okay?" Concerned, Nic reached out to steady his wife.

"I'm still trying to get my land legs," Millie said. "It takes a while for me to adjust to not being on board the ship."

"If it gets too bad, you can step outside and gaze at the horizon. It's worse in enclosed spaces," Regan said.

"Maybe we'll have to sleep on the porch," Millie joked.

The couples munched on an array of imported cheeses and crispy crackers while they caught up and made plans for Regan and Nadia to show Nic and Millie around the island. They also told the couple that they, along with their families, were free to use any of the water toys, boogie boards, snorkel gear and kayaks.

"Oh. I almost forgot to give them the wristbands." Nadia sprang from the chair and hurried to the kitchen. When she returned, she placed a container of bright blue wristbands on the table. "I grabbed a bunch, so there should be more than enough here for everyone. If not, let the front desk know and they'll give you more."

Regan glanced at his watch. "I need to get going. I have a meeting with all available employees in fifteen minutes to break the news about George and go over increased safety precautions."

"Me too." Nadia carried her empty drink glass to the kitchen and placed it inside the dishwasher. "This will give you two a chance to settle in and unpack. Oh, I also jotted down your children's room numbers. Their rooms are in the main building, close to all of the activities and the pools."

"For more privacy," Nic winked at Millie.

"Of course," Nadia's eyes twinkled with mischief. "We can't have them too close."

"Are you joining us for dinner this evening?" Millie asked.

Nadia and Regan exchanged a quick glance. "I'm sorry." Regan cleared his throat. "Our schedule was thrown off kilter today with the discovery of George's body and the police going over the place with a fine tooth comb. We'll get together another night."

"And since this is your last night with your children, we don't want to impose," Nadia chimed in.

"You're not imposing," Nic said. "But we understand if you have other obligations."

The couple walked Regan and Nadia to the front door and followed them out onto the front porch. A cool ocean breeze blew strands of Millie's hair across her face and she tucked them behind her ear.

Regan reached for his wife's hand and they started down the steps. "Oh. I almost forgot about the golf outing and golf tournament at Mullet Bay."

"Golf?" Millie asked.

"Regan invited me...I mean *us* to a golf outing on Wednesday and then to watch a golf tournament at the Mullet Bay Country Club on Friday," Nic said.

Millie's sharp eye didn't miss the glimmer of hope in Nic's eyes. He loved golf. In fact, he owned an expensive set of golf clubs, which sat collecting dust in his apartment. The only time he'd used them was when he attacked a passenger who attempted to hijack the Siren of the Seas.

"I'm not interested in going. I'm sure I can lounge by the pool, read a good book or two and enjoy some peace and quiet," Millie said. "But I want you to go. Have fun and enjoy yourself."

"I don't think I should go without you, especially seeing that this is our honeymoon."

Nadia lifted a hand. "Don't worry about Millie. Since Regan is taking some time off, I will as well. Perhaps Millie and I can plan a spa day. I've been dying to try La Patisserie. I heard they have chocolate croissants that are out of this world."

"I don't want to impose," Millie said.

"You're not imposing. It's settled then. A spa day and then La Patisserie and some downtown shopping are in order."

"But..." Millie still felt as if she was imposing.

"No 'buts' about it," Nadia smiled.

"It's useless to try to change Nadia's mind once she gets something stuck in her head," Regan said. "I'm sure the girls will have a ball."

"Then it's settled." Nadia turned to her husband. "What time are you leaving for the golf course on Wednesday?"

"Tee time is at ten," Regan said. "Why don't we all meet for breakfast at Water's Edge around a quarter to nine?"

"Perfect," Millie said as she slipped her hand in Nic's. "That will give us the rest of the day with our children and a day alone tomorrow before the golf outing."

"We'll have an entire weekend in paradise and then it's back to the Siren of the Seas," Nic finished.

"We just got here and the week is already half over," Millie joked.

"Which reminds me, we've got to head out." Regan and Nadia waved good-bye before stepping onto the paved path and disappearing from sight.

Nic placed an arm around his wife's shoulders. "What do you think of this place?"

"It's gorgeous," Millie said. "Living here would be like living in paradise. We should walk to the beach and check it out."

The couple quickly unpacked their suitcase, slipped on some flip-flops and then meandered down to the shoreline where they planned to meet up with all of the children to enjoy some time at the beach.

Millie gazed back at the cottage. "I can't believe how close we are to the ocean. Regan and Nadia gave us the best cottage at Grand Bay."

"I take it you like Nadia?"

"She's super sweet. We hit it off right away," Millie said. "She's a lot like me." She thought of Nadia's insistence that they were being followed and that the resort had been bugged with listening devices, but decided it was more of a quirk than a fault, and completely understandable considering the resort had three suspicious deaths.

Millie and Nic settled into a couple of empty lounge chairs to wait for the children. Blake and

Erin were the first to arrive. They chatted with Nic and Millie with Erin gushing over their room and the resort. Finally, they decided to walk along the shoreline and Nic and Millie were alone again.

Millie glanced toward the walkway, shading her eyes. "I hope Beth, David and the kids...and Fiona can make it."

"I...don't think Fiona will, but I see Beth and the family now," Nic said.

Bella and Noah ran ahead when they spotted their grandmother while the parents brought up the rear. "This place is so nice," Beth said. "What a beautiful beach." She cast a gaze at the water, gently lapping at the shoreline.

"Can we go swimming?" Noah tugged on his father's hand.

"Sure."

"Here. Everyone needs a wristband." Millie passed out the wristbands.

The children slipped them on and then darted to the water's edge with David following close behind.

Beth placed the beach towels on the sand and dropped a beach bag on top. She turned to Nic. "Thank you so much for including us. This has been one of the best vacations we've ever had. I think the kids are ready to move here."

"It is beautiful," Millie agreed.

Millie's grandchildren frolicked in the water, collected seashells on the beach and then headed to the snack shack for ice cream. By late afternoon, it was nap time, so Beth and David gathered their things and headed back to their room.

Blake and Erin left a short time later, promising to meet up with them for dinner.

"It's just the two of us again," Nic said. "Now it's our turn to walk the beach." The couple strolled to the water's edge where the warm Caribbean water lapped at the tips of Millie's toes.

"Regan told me that Nadia is gung-ho to figure out why people are being murdered here at the resort and when she found out you had a nose for tracking down killers, she couldn't wait for you to get here."

"She told me the same thing. No wonder I like her."

"Two peas in a pod," Nic said. "Did she give you the grand tour and show you where they found the bodies?"

Nic studied Millie's expression. "Ah. I can tell from the look on your face that she did. I'm sure you're dying to help your new friend, and I can't blame you. These are serious matters, which is why I think you should stay out of it. We're in a foreign country. All I need is for you to end up in a French prison and me trying to figure out how to get you out."

Millie splayed her hand across her chest. "Do you really think I would do something that would cause me to end up getting arrested?"

"Not on purpose, but once you start digging around, you plunge headfirst and consider the consequences later," Nic said.

"When was the last time I got in trouble?"

"Not long ago, when you went undercover, working in the maintenance department with Annette."

"Nothing happened," Millie insisted. "We didn't even find Isaac Risang's body. Someone else did."

"What about the time you were almost electrocuted on the new Killer Karaoke stage?"

"I realized something was wrong and called Marcus to fix it," Millie said.

Nic shook his head. "You are a stubborn woman."

"One of the many reasons you married me." Millie quickly changed the subject as she leaned down and wiggled a shell out of the sand, holding it up for inspection. "I think I'm going to start a shell collection and put them in an empty glass jar as a souvenir of our honeymoon."

The couple drifted along the water's edge, past the resort. They turned around when they reached a pile of boulders jutting out into the water.

Millie collected a few more shells on the return trip and by the time they reached the resort, she had a handful.

"Shall we go back to the room for a rest?" Nic raised a brow.

"I thought you'd never ask," Millie lowered her lids. "Did you see the Jacuzzi tub in the bathroom? We should give it a try."

"I was going to make the same suggestion."

***

"You look gorgeous." Nic kissed the back of his wife's neck. "And you smell wonderful. What is that?"

"It's a new perfume I picked up from Cat's gift shop. It's called Midnight Seductress."

"The name is fitting. The smell is tempting me...tempting me to show up late for dinner," Nic said. "How much time do we have before we have to leave?"

"Not enough," Millie said as she smoothed the edges of her silk blouse. "Maybe I should change."

"Why?" Nic snaked an arm around his wife and pulled her close. "It's just dinner with the kids."

"And my first time meeting Fiona," Millie said nervously.

"You worry too much. One day, Fiona will love you as much as I do."

"I'll settle for tolerating for the here and now," Millie groaned.

"Fiona is her own person. She likes to speak her mind and you'll know exactly where you stand with her from the moment you meet her."

"That makes me feel somewhat better…maybe," Millie tugged on the sleeve of her blouse. "I'm ready to head down there if you are."

Nic reached for Millie's hand and squeezed it tight. "It will be all right. Really, I promise it will. Be yourself and the rest will take care of itself."

Chapter 10

Nic had made dinner reservations at LeBistro, the upscale French restaurant near the back of the resort. It sported a magnificent view, overlooking the ocean.

Millie stopped near the entrance and clutched her chest, certain that at any moment she was going to have a heart attack. Looking back, she should've known Fiona had avoided meeting her for a reason. She didn't want her father to remarry and Nadia had confirmed Millie's fears.

What if Fiona hated her? What if she gave her father an ultimatum...Millie or her?

Beth, David and the kids, along with Blake and Erin would be there. Surely, the woman would not cause a scene in front of complete strangers.

Millie squared her shoulders and waited for Nic to open the door. "I love you," he whispered in her ear.

"I love you too."

Nic approached the hostess station. "Reservations for Armati, party of nine."

"Yes of course." The young woman smiled. "Follow me. One of the others in your party has already arrived." They made a beeline down a wide center aisle before zigzagging between several occupied tables.

The hostess waved her hand at the lone occupant and Millie forced herself to smile. Seated directly across from them was a woman. Mid-thirties if Millie had to guess. Her brown hair was chopped short, with stray wisps curling around her neck.

Millie would never have known the woman at the table was related to Nic if not for her eyes, which were the same brooding shade of dark brown. The woman didn't smile or even acknowledge Millie and instead focused her attention on Nic.

"Hello Father. It appears I'm the only one who is considerate enough to be punctual."

"We're only a couple of minutes late." Nic hurried around the table, to the woman's side, where he bent down and gave her a quick hug. "I trust you're feeling better?"

"I'm fine. In fact, I'm ready to go home. I tried to switch my flight to today, but departing flights are completely booked."

Nic straightened his back. "I'm glad you didn't leave." He motioned to Millie.

"Fiona, this is Millie. Millie...Fiona."

Millie circled the table, joined Nic and extended her hand.

Fiona stared at Millie's outstretched hand and scowled.

Millie awkwardly dropped her hand. "It's so nice to finally meet you," she said. "I love your hair. It's the perfect style for this Caribbean heat."

Fiona ignored Millie's compliment. "I already checked out the menu. Nothing looks appealing, except for the grilled cheese sandwich on the children's menu."

Nic pulled out an empty chair for Millie. "Would you like to have a seat?"

"Thank you." Millie eased into the empty chair while Nic sat in the one next to her, sandwiched between his daughter and new wife.

Thankfully, a server approached, carrying a pitcher of water. "Good evening Mr. Armati. Mr. Leclerc said I'm to treat you like royalty tonight and that you're here on your honeymoon."

Fiona snorted.

"Fiona," Nic warned.

"Would you care for something to drink?"

"I'll stick with water," Millie said.

"I will, as well," Nic replied. "What would you like Fiona?"

"I'll take a scotch on the rocks. Make it a double. If I can't find anything worth eating, at least I can drink."

"As you wish." The server departed, passing by Beth, David and the children as they made their way over.

Millie almost burst into tears at the sight of welcoming, familiar faces. She wiggled out of her chair and hugged her daughter. "You look beautiful."

"Thanks." Beth patted her husband's arm. "After the kids' naps, David took us shopping in Marigot and bought me this sundress."

"And Daddy got me a new dress too." Bella twirled in a circle to show her grandmother her new outfit.

Millie hugged her grandchildren and then David. "Do you like the resort?"

"It's magnificent," Beth gushed. "If we'd known how spectacular it was, we would've squeezed in a few extra nights."

"You should've seen it a couple of years ago. It was top notch," Fiona said. "The place is turning into a dump."

"Fiona," Nic chided. "This is a five star resort and exceptionally nice."

Blake and Erin arrived moments later and Millie hugged them both. "How is your room?"

"Perfect," Erin said. "We loved hanging out at the beach earlier, but haven't had a chance to check out the pools yet. We're going to head over there after dinner, right Blake?"

Erin didn't give Blake a chance to answer. "I forgot to mention this earlier. We had a little snafu leaving the ship. Blake forgot our backpack with our laptops, tablets and my e-reader inside the cabin. I think his name was Suhoo. He had to go back to our cabin to get it since we'd already left the ship and dropped off our keycards."

"Suharto," Nic said. "I'm glad you remembered before you left the dock area."

"I don't go anywhere without my tablet and e-reader," Erin said as she picked up the menu.

The server returned with Fiona's drink and placed it in front of her. Fiona lifted the glass, chugged the contents and set the empty glass on the table. "I'll take another one when you come back this way."

The server nodded. "What would you ladies and gentlemen like?"

After jotting down their drink orders, the server left the table and Erin picked up where she left off. "I'm taking a class on social media marketing. Someday, I would like to run an online business related to the veterinary field. Maybe start an online vet website and 24-hour hotline for people who are unable to get their pets to a physical location."

She rattled on about her class before seamlessly switching the topic to the cruise ship and the wedding. "It was a beautiful wedding. The food was so good. I never realized cruise ship food could be that good." Erin patted her stomach. "I probably gained five pounds. The Mexican fiesta was my favorite."

Erin took a breather when the server returned with their drinks and Fiona's second scotch on the rocks. She sipped the second drink a little more slowly and Millie began to relax.

Although the menu was limited, everything sounded delicious. Millie ordered the pan-seared halibut with mushrooms and fingerling potatoes. Each of them ordered a different dish and the children, along with Fiona, ordered the children's grilled cheese sandwich.

Thankfully, after Fiona polished off her second drink, she didn't order a third, but sat and stared, or more like glared…at everyone at the table.

"I don't think I've ever had Chilean sea bass before. It's not bad," Erin said. "It could use a little more salt."

Fed up, Fiona dropped her napkin on her plate and leaned forward. "Do you ever shut up?"

Erin's eyes widened and she let out a small whimper as she stared at Fiona.

"That was uncalled for," Nic said in a hard voice.

"It was exactly what was called for," Fiona gritted out. "The woman hasn't stopped jabbering about nothing since the moment she arrived. I thought this whole dinner was going to be a flop and I was right." She shoved her chair back and stood.

Nic stood. "You owe everyone here, especially Erin, an apology."

"Oh, I do?" Fiona stuck her hand on her hip. "Even your precious bride? I have no idea what you see in her. She's not even pretty." Fiona didn't wait for a reply and stomped out of the restaurant.

"I'm so sorry," Nic apologized before chasing after his daughter.

"Good riddance," Beth muttered. "What a witch."

"At least you don't have to see her very often," Blake said.

Millie turned to Erin. "I am so sorry Erin."

"It's okay. I know I talk a lot, but it's usually only when I get nervous...you know, meeting you for the first time and then your husband. I'm sorry if I rambled on."

"You're fine." Millie patted her hand. "I believe Fiona's goal may have been to cause a scene."

"She did a great job." David lifted his glass. "I propose a toast."

Millie lifted her glass.

"A toast to a peaceful rest of the evening."

The group clinked glasses and conversation began to flow with Erin chiming in every now and then, but not monopolizing the conversation as she'd previously done.

Nic didn't return for the remainder of the meal, so Millie asked the server to box his food. He returned when the dessert arrived, his expression pinched. "I would like to apologize again for my daughter's behavior. I have no excuse."

"It's okay Nic. I'm sure Fiona is going through a period of adjustment," Beth said graciously.

"Yeah," Erin nodded. "I talk too much when I'm stressed out. Maybe she just gets angry."

Nic settled back into his chair and Millie patted his leg under the table. At least their first meeting was over and Millie knew exactly where she stood with Nic's daughter.

Millie sipped her cup of coffee and gazed at her children with pride. Sure, it was an emotional time watching their mother marry again, knowing she chose to live on board a cruise ship and that she would never return to Michigan full-time, at least not for several more years.

The couple had mulled over retiring someday and splitting their time between Italy and Michigan. They both owned their homes outright, giving them an opportunity to enjoy the best of both worlds.

They still had a number of details to work out and they decided to discuss it again, a few years down the road. They were both in good health, with many years of adventures ahead of them aboard the Siren of the Seas, with Majestic Cruise Lines.

God had been good to Millie Sanders...now Millie Armati. He had given her a wonderful life, a loving husband and family.

There wasn't anything else she could think of that she needed or even wanted. All Millie held dear was sitting around the table.

Nic attempted to pay the bill for dinner and the waiter reminded him it was an all-inclusive resort. "I'm going to have to pay Regan and Nadia back for inviting us to stay here."

"All of us," Millie said. "Nadia told me she and Regan are joining us later this year for a cruise.

The group assembled outside the restaurant and Millie's throat clogged as she hugged each of her children and grandchildren. It was hard saying good-bye, but she swallowed the lump in her throat and forced a smile.

"Please call me when you make it home," she said.

"We will," Beth promised.

Nic and Millie stood on the sidewalk, waiting for the family to disappear inside the lobby of the hotel when the sound of sirens filled the air.

Several fire trucks roared onto the main street and came to a screeching halt near the front lobby doors.

Chapter 11

"Uh-oh," Millie said. "There's smoke coming from the kitchen area."

Several firefighters, dressed in full gear, dragged water hoses to the back of the building.

Nic and Millie made their way closer and the acrid smell of smoke wafted in the air.

An emergency vehicle pulled in next to one of the fire trucks. Two women sprang from the ambulance and jogged to the back of the building.

Millie took a tentative step forward, her heart pounding loudly as one of the firefighters shook his head. A second firefighter emerged from the building and motioned the EMTs inside. "Someone must've gotten hurt."

The crowd grew quiet, as if holding a collective breath, and watched as one of the EMTs returned to the ambulance, rolled a stretcher from the back and carried it inside.

"I hope it's not Nadia or Regan." Millie watched as a firefighter pulled the hose to the side of the firetruck and began rolling it up. "It looks as if the fire is out."

Moments later, the ambulance workers exited the back of the building, carrying the stretcher. Lying on the stretcher was a young woman. Her hand was wrapped in a bandage and there was another, larger one wrapped around her upper leg. She was alert and said something to the workers, but Millie wasn't close enough to hear.

The EMTs eased the stretcher into the back of the ambulance before closing the doors and climbing into the cab. They drove onto the road and silently sped off.

Moments later, Regan emerged from the back of the building and stood talking to one of the firefighters, a grim expression on his face.

"Poor Regan and Nadia," Nic murmured.

"Something fishy is going on here," Millie said.

"I agree. No one can have that much bad luck. It looks as if the poor young woman on the stretcher was almost victim number four."

"There's nothing we can do here tonight," Nic continued. "We'll check on Regan and Nadia first thing in the morning."

Millie contemplated the string of events and everything Nadia had told her as the couple silently made their way to the cottage. Was Regan's bitter ex-partner trying to ruin his business and destroy his life? The partner would certainly be familiar with the resort's layout.

Surely, the authorities would be looking closely at the partner, Wayne Clemson. If Clemson was behind the deaths, was he dumb enough to keep up with the criminal activities and murders in the midst of more than one open investigation?

Perhaps it was Ellen Fulbright's husband; trying to throw the authorities off, making it look like someone inside the resort...a worker...had murdered his wife. If so, he was going to a lot of trouble to cast suspicion on someone else, but then again, if he had been responsible for his wife's death, he was trying to get away with murder.

Millie made a mental note to ask Nadia if the Fulbrights had toured the kitchen or taken the cooking class. Raoul had died after being trapped inside the walk-in freezer and now this...two of the four incidents had occurred in the main building's kitchen area.

When they reached the cottage, Nic finally spoke. "I want to make sure the cottage is empty before we both go inside. "Better safe than sorry." He scanned his keycard and disappeared inside the cottage. The flicker of light from a tableside lamp near the window cast a warm glow onto the porch.

A short time later, Nic emerged from the cottage and stepped out onto the porch. "The coast is clear. No one is lurking inside."

"That's a relief." Millie sank into the rocker next to the door. It was a shame that such a magnificent slice of paradise had turned deadly. If things kept up, no one would want to stay at Grand Bay Beach Club, and who could blame them?

What if it was a competitor, trying to drive them out of business? Millie's list of questions for Nadia was adding up.

Nic slipped past his wife, eased into the rocking chair next to her and gazed out at the ocean. "I'm know Nadia and you spoke about the recent string of deaths. Did she give you any clue as to who might be behind them?"

"Yes." Millie tapped her sandal on the porch floor and the chair began to rock. "Regan is embroiled in a bitter lawsuit with his ex-partner, Wayne Clemson."

"Regan mentioned Wayne Clemson's name to me, as well," Nic changed the subject. "I want to apologize again for Fiona's behavior at dinner this evening. I guess I didn't realize the depth of her anger over her mother's death." He sighed. "I tried to talk to her after her outburst and she went off on me."

Millie reached over and grasped Nic's hand. "Time heals all wounds; at least that's what they say. I'm sure the thought of us marrying was difficult, especially considering Fiona doesn't see you often. She probably views me as an outsider, someone who is taking even more of her father's time and she's lashing out."

Nic slowly nodded. "You're probably right." He shifted in the chair and gazed thoughtfully at his bride. "What did I ever do to deserve you?"

"I'll take that as a compliment." Millie slid out of the rocker. "It has been a long day and I'm whupped."

"It has been a long day." Nic followed his wife to the door and then inside the cottage. "I've got a big day planned for us tomorrow."

"Oh?" Millie abruptly stopped. "What plans?"

"It's a surprise. You'll have to wait and see."

***

Millie Sanders-Armati placed a hand on her hip and frowned at her husband. "Where did you say you were taking me?"

"I didn't," Nic said. "Today's adventure involves water, so you'll need to change into your bathing suit while I run over to the pool's snack shack and grab something. I also want to stop at the main building to see if I can track down Regan to find out what happened with the firetrucks and ambulance last night." He turned to go and then turned back. "We'll also need some sunscreen, bug spray and a couple of beach towels."

Before Millie could say another word, he traipsed out of the cottage, humming a catchy tune as he sauntered down the path toward the pool area.

Millie packed a beach bag with the items Nic mentioned, changed into her bathing suit and grabbed a couple of beach towels. She zipped the bag shut and carried it into the living room when she heard heavy steps on the front porch.

Nic opened the door and stepped into the living room. "What a mess."

"You mean the fire last night?" Millie asked.

"Yeah. Regan is beside himself." Nic glanced at his watch. "We better get going. I'll tell you what happened later."

Millie gathered the towels and beach bag and joined Nic on the porch.

"Do you have your sunglasses?" Nic tapped his glasses, perched atop his head.

"No." Millie ran back indoors, returning moments later with her sunglasses.

"Perfect. Let's go." Nic switched the soft side cooler to his other shoulder and reached for Millie's hand. "What's with the gloomy face? You look as if I'm leading you to a firing squad."

"I wasn't too concerned until you mentioned bug spray. Have I ever told you I have an aversion to spiders?"

"As much as you do to elevators?" he teased.

"Yeah, critters are a close second."

"I'll keep that in mind." They stepped onto the walkway leading to the beach and stopped when they reached the end. "Over there." Nic pointed to the beach shack, not far from where they stood.

Millie frowned. "What's over there?"

"Clear kayaks," Nic said. "We're going kayaking. I found out that there are several small, secluded beaches not far from here. I thought we could take some snorkel gear, too."

"Great," Millie groaned. "I've only tried snorkeling once, so you're gonna have to rescue me if I start going under."

"Not likely," Nic shook his head. "You'll float in the seawater, not to mention we'll be wearing life jackets."

The couple made their way over to the stand and Millie waited off to the side. Nic handed her two life jackets and then pick up the bag of snorkel gear.

The man inside the shack stepped out of the small building, grabbed a paddle propped up against the side of the building and then led them to a kayak. "This is the clear kayak you'll be using. Even if you don't see much while snorkeling, you should be able to spot some fish and other sea life through the bottom of the kayak."

"What kind of sea life?" Visions of sharks with sharp teeth filled Millie's head.

"The usual…stingrays, eels, maybe even an octopus if you're lucky."

"I hope not."

"Give it a chance," Nic said. "You might find you like it."

"You're right. I don't mean to be a party pooper." Millie set her beach bag on the sand and pulled the life jacket on.

Nic slipped his on and then set the cooler in the back of the kayak. "We can put the beach bag and snorkel gear in the front to balance it out."

"I'll push you into open water," the man said. "Steer clear of the rocks. If you get too close, you'll get hung up on them."

"Thanks for the warning."

"You want a paddle mum?"

"Sure." Millie climbed into the kayak and plopped down on the plastic bench.

The worker ran back to the shed, returned with a second paddle and handed it to Millie.

"Thanks. I think."

"You get in now," the man motioned to Nic.

Nic rolled into the kayak and crawled to the bench seat while the man gave the kayak a sharp shove and it slipped into the open water.

It took a few moments for the couple to get the hang of maneuvering the small craft. Nic stayed near the shoreline without getting too close and Millie began to relax as they paddled in rhythm.

The couple took turns pointing out the various brightly colored fish that swam under the kayak. They continued paddling along the shoreline until Millie spotted a cove and a small sandy beach. "I see a beach."

"I think this is the one the employee at the shack told me about." The couple steered the kayak toward shore. When they got close, Nic jumped out and pulled it onto the beach. "This oughta do it."

"Perfect." Millie handed him the snorkel gear and cooler before climbing out. "Scout would love playing in this sand and splashing around in the water." A tinge of sadness filled Millie as she thought about their small pooch.

"We'll bring him one day." Nic unzipped the cooler, reached inside and removed two bottled waters. He handed one to Millie. "It's going to be a scorcher today."

"Thank you. At least the ocean breezes make it more tolerable." Millie sipped her water before replacing the lid. "What else is inside the cooler?"

"Lunch. I hope you like what I picked out."

"I'm sure I will," Millie settled onto her towel and Nic joined her. He reached inside the cooler and pulled out a plastic container. "There are grilled chicken wraps, cut fruit, some chips and cookies for dessert."

Millie unwrapped the wraps and handed one to Nic. They joined hands and Nic began to pray. "Lord, thank you for this beautiful day. Thank you for my beautiful new wife. Please bless our marriage, give us a week filled with memories and moments we can treasure forever. Thank you for this food. Amen."

"Amen," Millie leaned over and kissed her husband. "You're so sweet. I love you."

"I love you too." Nic held out the container of fruit and Millie reached for a piece of pineapple. The juicy tart fruit nearly melted in her mouth. "This is delicious. What a beautiful day. You picked the perfect outing."

"Thank you and I agree," Nic nodded. "The only thing making it less than perfect is poor Regan and Nadia's situation."

"That's right. You said you talked to Regan this morning. What happened last night?"

"It's still too early to tell, but Regan thinks someone tampered with the gas lines in the kitchen, causing a small explosion."

Chapter 12

"Tampered with the gas lines in the kitchen?" Millie gasped.

"Alyssa, a kitchen worker, was getting ready to swap out one of the propane tanks. She thought she turned it off, but instead, turned it on high. The fire chief believes a spark may have caused an explosion and a stack of cardboard boxes nearby caught on fire."

Nic continued. "The employee tried to put the fire out and ended up getting burned."

"So this time there's a chance it truly was an accident," Millie said.

"Maybe," Nic shrugged. "Just as it may have been an accident Raoul got trapped in the walk-in freezer."

Millie reached for a chocolate macadamia nut cookie, broke off a large piece and chewed thoughtfully. "She's lucky she's alive."

"Yes, she is. I guess we missed the news crews. They arrived en masse and the story is all over the local news."

"How convenient. I'm sure the whole island knows about the other incidents, as well."

"The authorities showed up this morning while I was there. Regan is concerned the local agency, the one governing commercial kitchens, is going to shut them down pending an investigation."

"A valid concern," Millie said. "I think Grand Bay is being sabotaged, which makes me wonder if a competitor is trying to destroy their reputation and ruin their business."

"Although it's a sad situation, there's nothing you or I can do at the moment," Nic said. "Let's try to enjoy the rest of our afternoon. We can talk about it later."

"I agree." Millie packed up the leftovers and set the cooler off to the side before grabbing a tube of sunscreen and slathering a thick layer on her exposed skin.

"While you relax I'm going to scope out the snorkeling." Nic reached inside the snorkel bag and pulled out a set of fins, goggles and a snorkel tube.

He slipped the fins over the top of his water shoes and plodded to the water's edge where he tugged the mask over his head and adjusted it before hooking the snorkel tube. He turned back and gave Millie a nod before easing deeper into the water.

Millie kept a close eye on the tip of the snorkel tube and Nic's fins until he rounded a cluster of rocks and disappeared from sight.

She scrambled to her feet and made her way to the water's edge where she spotted her husband in open water. Millie waded into the warm

Caribbean waters and a small school of fish promptly circled her ankles.

Millie scooped her hand into the water to try to catch one of the fish, but they were quick and easily darted away. A movement in the water caught her eye and she watched as Nic trekked to shore. When he got close, he plopped down in the shallow water and removed the fins.

"How was it?"

"Good. Not great. I could see as much through the bottom of the kayak as I could while snorkeling." He turned to face his wife and the shoreline. "Would you like to give it a try?

Millie almost said "no" until she noted the hopeful look in Nic's eyes. "Sure. You'll have to give me a few pointers."

"Of course."

"I'll go get the other snorkel gear." Millie waded to shore and made her way over to the snorkel bag. She removed the second set of snorkel gear and headed back to the water. It took several minutes for Nic to help her "gear up" and then they hung around the shallow water so that Millie could practice.

At first, Millie panicked when she realized her only air supply was through the snorkel tube and her claustrophobia threatened to kick into high gear. It took several tries for her to get the hang of breathing through the mouthpiece. "I think I'm ready."

Nic led her into the deeper water, promising to stay close by. Millie adjusted the gear and stuck her face in the water, her body floating face down. Her first instinct was to gasp for air, but she forced herself to remain calm and focus on the beauty of the creatures and the colorful coral reef.

It worked and soon Millie was paddling around, chasing after the colorful fish. Some were round with black stripes while others were silver with patches of yellow along their sides and near their fins, but her favorites were the blue ones.

Nic swam to his wife's side and pushed the snorkel tube from his mouth. "It's getting late and we still have to kayak back to the resort."

Millie nodded. "I'll follow you." When they reached the shallow water, she flipped over and removed her fins as she'd seen Nic do earlier.

"Well? What did you think?" Nic asked.

"It was amazing," Millie said. "God's beautiful creatures. Thank you for talking me into giving snorkeling another try."

"So you'll go again?"

"Yes. It was fun." After rinsing the sand out of the snorkel gear and fins, Millie placed everything back into the bag while Nic shook the sand from their beach towels and shoved them, along with the sunscreen, in the bag.

"Do you have your cell phone?" Nic asked.

"I do." Millie unzipped the pocket of the bag, reached inside and pulled out her cell phone.

"Let's try this selfie thing."

Millie switched the phone on, pressed the camera button and the couple moved close together. Her first picture was a clear shot of the tops of their heads, but the second attempt was much better.

After taking several pictures, Millie snapped a few more of their private beach area and then put her phone back in the bag while Nic loaded the rest of their stuff into the kayak.

"Ready?"

"Yeah." Millie glanced back wistfully at their secluded slice of paradise. The day was turning out to be one of the least stressful days she'd had in weeks.

The memory of Fiona's uncomfortable outburst was forgotten as Millie climbed into the kayak. Nic gave it a quick shove and vaulted over the side.

Millie grinned. "You're getting pretty good at that."

"Not bad for an old man."

"You're – we're not old, just aged, like fine wine." Millie grabbed the paddle and the couple steered the kayak along the shoreline, retracing their path to the resort. The return trip seemed quicker and Millie suspected it was because she was more confident in her kayaking abilities.

The young man who had sent them off waded into the water, grabbed the tip of the kayak and pulled it onto the beach. When they reached knee-deep water, Millie hopped out to lighten the load and the men finished pulling it onto the sand.

"How was it?"

"Wonderful," Millie gushed. "This was my first attempt at kayaking and my second attempt at snorkeling, all in one day."

"Ah mum. You had a good time then?"

"Yes. It was perfect."

After returning all of the snorkel gear, the life jackets and the kayak paddles, the couple strolled along the shoreline as they made their way back to the cottage.

Nic squeezed his wife's hand. "What would you like to do for dinner? We could explore the island and find a nice beachfront restaurant."

"True, but it's a shame since all of the meals at the resort are included," Millie said.

"I don't want you to feel like you're being shortchanged."

"Not at all." Millie shook her head. "I would be happy eating here. I noticed on the schedule of events that they have live music after seven. I'm not really hungry right now, so if you're okay with it we can wait until later to go down."

"Sounds good to me." The couple turned onto the path leading to the cottage. "Don't forget, we'll be meeting Regan and Nadia for breakfast in the morning and then Regan and I are heading to the golf outing."

"I think Nadia has taken care of plans for the two of us to do something," Millie said. "She mentioned a spa day and perhaps checking out a French bakery."

They reached the porch and Nic set the beach bag next to the door. "Are you sure you don't mind me going to the golf outing? I'll be going to the tournament later in the week, as well."

"This is both our honeymoon and vacation. Go. Have a good time. Enjoy your rounds of golf. We still have all week to explore the island and spend time alone, like we did today."

"If you're sure." Nic swiped his card and opened the cottage door.

"I'll shake the towels again later and hang them on the rockers to dry," Millie said. "I don't want to track sand in here."

Millie offered to let Nic shower first since it would take her longer to primp and get ready. She settled onto a barstool and switched the television on to search for a local weather report.

She flipped through the channels, searching for a local station when one of the reports caught her eye. It was a clip of the resort's kitchen fire the previous night. Millie turned the volume up, hopped off the stool and made her way to the television for a closer look.

"...suspicious explosion at the five star Grand Bay Beach Club resort. The resort's employee, Alyssa Durand, is still in the hospital, recovering from burns to her leg and hand. The doctors expect a full recovery and the woman should be released from the hospital at any time."

The reporter mentioned Raoul's death, George's death and Ellen's death.

"The local authorities are searching for clues to see if there are links between the recent deaths and last evening's explosion."

The reporter turned to his co-anchor and tapped his stack of papers on top of the news desk. "It appears that Grand Bay is either very unlucky or something more sinister is taking place."

"I would agree with you there, Arlyn. Now onto other island news."

Nic emerged from the bedroom, drying his hair. "Well? Is my golf outing going to be a washout?"

Millie set the remote on the coffee table. "I'm beginning to think you don't want to go golfing."

"I do," Nic said. "I'm still feeling guilty."

"Well don't. I'm sure I'll have a wonderful time hanging out with Nadia and doing girl stuff. Maybe I'll spring for a full massage."

"Just make sure it's not some hot hunk giving the massage," Nic teased.

"Good grief. That should be the least of your worries." Millie rolled her eyes and headed to the bathroom. While she showered, Millie thought of the string of tragedies at the resort. She was sure there was some sort of connection. It wasn't bad luck. It was something else. Maybe Regan's former business partner was behind the deaths and the explosion.

Perhaps tomorrow, Nadia and she could put their heads together and start assembling the clues. Showering always cleared the cobwebs and as Millie lathered her hair, it dawned on her there were clues, right in front of her eyes...something that might point Nadia and Millie in the right direction.

Chapter 13

While Millie and Nic waited in the front lobby the next morning for Nadia and Regan, they admired the aerial photos of the resort hanging on the wall. In one, a couple was parasailing, high above the mesmerizing turquoise waters. "Better them than me," Millie muttered under her breath.

"I guess parasailing is out," Nic said.

A small commotion near a side door caught Millie's attention. Regan and Nadia were huddled close, talking to a man dressed in a bellhop uniform. The employee nodded glumly and then walked away without saying a word.

Millie caught Nadia's eye and the couple made their way over.

"Is everything okay?"

"Yes. We were discussing a minor incident with an employee," Regan said.

"Minor?" Nadia said. "Dennis needs to learn to keep his hands to himself." She turned to Nic and Millie. "Two of our female wait staff complained he was making suggestive comments and they were uncomfortable. This is his last warning."

"He's fully aware of how you feel," Regan said.

"We can't risk a sexual harassment suit. We have enough problems right now."

"I couldn't agree more. Let's not air our dirty laundry," Regan said lightly. "Shall we head to the restaurant?"

During breakfast, the couples compared life on board a cruise ship versus life in a beach resort. There were some similarities...new names and faces on a consistent basis, working long hours to ensure beach guests and cruise ship guests were happy, not to mention sometimes feeling like you're living in a bubble.

The more Millie learned about Regan and Nadia, the more she liked them, and could see how Nic and Regan had formed a close friendship. They were a lot alike.

Millie thought of how close she'd grown to Annette, Cat and Danielle, not to mention Andy. During her marriage to Roger, her world revolved around their business, Central Michigan Private Investigators, and Roger.

Of course, she had friends from church and neighbors she considered friends, but nothing like the ones on the Siren of the Seas, the down in the trenches, I've-got-your-back friends. It was clear Nadia could become one of those friends and Millie was grateful to have met her.

The men headed out while the women lingered over a cup of coffee. "Are you still up for a pampering at the spa? We have one here, but I'm always open to checking out the competition and there are a couple of day spas not far from here. One is in Saint-Martin and there a couple closer to Philipsburg, in St. Maarten."

"I'll let you decide," Millie said. "I've never been to a spa. The closest I've come is acupuncture."

Nadia snorted. "Acupuncture?"

"It's a long story and involves my boss, Andy Walker, who wanted me to get an inside scoop on the ship's acupuncturist." Millie shivered as she remembered Stephen Chow's needles. "Don't worry, I paid Andy back."

The women chatted about Millie and Nic's snorkeling and kayaking adventure, as well as the live music and dinner the previous evening.

Nadia pushed her chair back. "We could sit here all day and chat, but we've got places to go, massages to meet."

Millie downed the last of her coffee and stood. "I'm ready. Before we go, I wondered if you had a chance to take a look at the local news footage of the fire the other evening."

"No." Nadia frowned. "Was it bad? Did they say what an unsafe place Grand Bay Beach Club was?"

"It wasn't the most flattering footage," Millie admitted, "That's not why I'm asking. I suspect the gas leak is related to the recent deaths and you know how they say the criminal always returns to the scene of the crime. I thought it might be helpful if you took a look at the news clips to see if anything pops out at you."

"I hadn't thought of that. I'm sure the story is all over the internet." Nadia motioned her toward the exit. "We can stop by my place to check it out."

Regan and Nadia's home, a beach cottage similar to the one Nic and Millie were staying in, sported the exact same layout and décor and the only difference Millie could see was that it was larger. "What a beautiful home."

"Thanks." Nadia waited until Millie stepped inside before closing the door and locking it. "It's a little larger than the cottage you're staying in. We have two bedrooms and two baths. I decorated all of the cottages in what I like to call 'shabby seaside chic.'"

"I love the look. Do you mind if I steal it? Nic's apartment is...shall we say...mostly masculine."

"It could use a woman's touch," Nadia suggested.

"Definitely." Millie plucked her cell phone from her purse and snapped several photos of the cottage's interior. "Did you find the furnishings and décor here on the island?"

"Most of it, although some had to be imported." Nadia lowered her voice. "I'm not into the French look, so most of it came from the United States."

"Your secret is safe with me." Millie snapped a final photo of the kitchen and then dropped her phone inside her purse.

"Let me grab my computer." Nadia unplugged the laptop and carried it to the bar area. "We'll have more room if we sit at the bar."

Millie hopped up on a barstool and Nadia joined her. After logging in, Nadia typed in *Explosion at Grand Bay Beach Club* and a news clip popped up on the screen. "The video looks fairly short." She double-clicked on the link and a news video began to play, minus the sound.

"Whoops." Nadia turned the sound on and leaned forward. It was the same one Millie had watched the previous night. After it finished, Nadia swiped at a tear that trickled down her cheek. "I not only feel responsible for Alyssa's injuries, but also Raoul, George and Ellen's deaths."

Millie patted her arm. "You didn't harm those people, but someone did and we need to figure out who. Was there anyone or anything in the video that stood out?"

"I was so horrified by what the reporter said I wasn't paying attention. Let me watch it again." Nadia enlarged the screen and replayed the video. "There!" Nadia tapped the computer screen. "See the guy in the golf cart, off to the side? I think that's Salvatore Milner. Although I've never met him, I would bet money on it."

"Who is Salvatore Milner?"

"Milner is one of our competitors. He bought the old Bayside Resort down the street and fixed it up." She reduced the screen and opened another screen before typing in 'Salvatore Milner, Bayside Resort.'

Several results popped up and Nadia clicked on the top one. She scrolled through the screen, stopping when she reached a photo of a man. "Check it out. Salvatore purchased and renovated a run-down resort down the street. He's copying everything we do, from our happy hours and prices, to our guest appreciation program." Nadia wrinkled her nose. "He even added a putting green. If Regan finds out, he'll be green with envy since we don't have one. Get it…green?"

"Haha. Good one." Millie slipped her reading glasses on and studied the man's face. "Let's take another look at the image from the other night."

Nadia switched screens and zoomed in on the golf cart. The men looked a lot alike. "You're right," Millie said. "It could very well be the same man."

She leaned closer and tapped the screen. "There's an emblem on the side of the cart. It looks like a crescent beach."

"Good eye, Millie. The emblem looks exactly like this one." She switched back to the other screen and a shot of the competitor's resort. In front of the resort was a sign sporting a crescent, sandy beach. "I never considered Salvatore as a suspect. The resort hasn't been open long. He put a ton of money into the place, but it's not nearly as busy as we are. Of course, it's taken us years to build our following and it will take him a while to build his up."

"It would happen a whole lot faster if the guests who loved to stay in this area and at Grand Bay were scared off by the recent string of deaths and accidents," Millie said. "How much do you know about the man?"

"Nothing," Nadia said. "Other than he offers the same all-inclusive package and the same pay-per-perk services we do."

"Including a spa?"

Nadia slowly turned to Millie. "Including a spa."

"You said you've never met Salvatore Milner, right?"

"Right."

"So guess where I think we should go for our spa treatment."

"You read my mind." Nadia closed the lid on the laptop. "Won't it look suspicious, us walking up to the resort without a car and telling them we want to check out their spa services?"

"Not necessarily," Millie said. "I have a plan. Let's go."

Nadia locked the cottage door. "We can walk to Bayside. It's not far."

Thankfully, the sidewalk leading to the front of the resort was lined with palm trees, shading the women from the direct sunlight.

Despite the shade, Millie swiped at the beads of sweat that quickly formed on her forehead. "I should've brought a hat."

"It's hot," Nadia agreed. "Thanks for helping me out, Millie."

"You're welcome Nadia. I only hope we'll stumble upon something that leads us in the right direction," Millie said. "So now we have two suspects…Regan's former partner."

"Wayne Clemson."

"Right. Wayne Clemson and Salvatore Milner."

"And perhaps Gordy Fulbright," Nadia said. "We're almost there."

The women rounded a sharp bend and a familiar sign with a crescent moon logo came into view. Below the logo was the name *Bayside Resort*. At the very bottom of the sign was a flashing neon "vacancy" light.

"Here goes nothing." Nadia marched into the lobby and Millie trailed behind.

"Can I help you?"

"Yes. We were wondering about your spa services and the hours."

"The spa is open now." The woman reached behind the counter and pulled out two sheets of paper, sliding one in front of Nadia and the other in front of Millie. "Have you been here before?"

"No," Nadia said. "This is our first time."

"Perfect." The woman beamed. "Let me have one of our staff give you a tour of the spa area." She picked up a two-way radio. "Janice. Could you please come to the front desk? We have visitors who would like a tour of the Serenity Spa." She set the radio down. "Janice will be here in a moment. Are you staying nearby?"

"Next door," Nadia blurted out.

"At the Grand Bay Beach Club," Millie said smoothly. "We'll be here until Monday."

The woman lifted a brow. "You didn't care for Grand Bay's spa?"

"We thought we would try something different today," Nadia said.

Millie leaned an elbow on the counter and shook her head. "It's such a shame about the recent deaths at the resort."

The woman tsk-tsked. "Yes. Grand Bay is one of the most popular resorts on the island and has a five star rating. It's hard to find a vacancy at the resort in high season, but that may all change now. We've had several bookings lately, from guests who previously stayed at Grand Bay, but are now concerned about the recent string of tragic events," she smirked.

Nadia's eyes narrowed and she opened her mouth to blast the woman with a snappy reply.

Millie noted the look on Nadia's face and quickly intervened. "I'm sure the authorities will quickly apprehend the criminal or criminals who are targeting Grand Bay."

"Are you here for a spa tour?" A petite redhead joined the trio.

"They are," the desk clerk nodded.

"Perfect." The woman tapped the top of her name tag. "My name is Janice and I'll be taking you on the tour. Are you staying at our resort?"

"No. We're staying at Grand Bay." Nadia shot the desk clerk a death look and Millie nudged her, silently shaking her head.

Janice led them to the end of a long corridor where they turned left, passing by a row of windows and an indoor pool. When they reached the end of the second corridor, their tour guide abruptly stopped. She scanned her keycard and pushed open the door.

The main spa area was spacious and ultra-modern, and Millie grudgingly admitted it was nice.

Janice pointed toward a curtained area, off to one side. "Over here, we offer an aquatic spa treatment."

"That sounds intriguing," Millie said.

"It's one of our most popular treatments. The therapist guides you to your pool suite before gently stretching your body, all the while simultaneously applying acupressure," Janice said. "It's like floating while doing yoga."

Millie's hand flew to her chest. "Acupuncture?"

"Acupressure," Nadia and Janice said in unison.

"Two completely different things," Nadia reassured her friend. She turned to the woman. "What do you offer as far as a total massage?"

"I recommend the Amazing Azure. This treatment incorporates a jade stone footbath. The full-body massage uses warm and cool jade stones to release tension. If you're stressed out, you won't be after this massage."

Janice led them to a reception desk near the front of the spa area. "We have two openings right now. If you decide to use our services, you'll not only receive a discount if you both choose a treatment, you'll also get an extra 10% off for being a first time customer, unlike some of the other spas in the area."

"Such as Grand Bay Beach Club?" Nadia asked.

"Yes," Janice nodded. "Although their treatment facilities are comparable to ours, they don't offer the first time discount like we do. It can save quite a bit of money."

"You seem to know a lot about other area spas," Millie commented.

"Of course." Janice smiled smugly. "One must always check out the competition."

"You've got that right," Nadia mumbled under her breath.

"Would you like to go ahead with the treatments?"

"No," Millie said.

"Yes," Nadia said. "My treat." She reached for her wallet and then realized if she handed the woman her credit card, she would see that Nadia was Nadia Leclerc. Her eyes widened and Millie realized why.

"My treat, N...Nancy," she quickly covered. "I'll take the aquatic treatment and I think you should try the Amazing Azure, so we can compare the two."

"R-right," Nadia stuttered. "Thanks, Millie."

"You're welcome. I owe you one. Actually, more than one." Millie handed the woman her credit card.

Janice rang up the treatments and handed Millie her card and a receipt.

Millie glanced at the receipt before shoving it in her front pocket. The prices were in line with the cruise ship spa prices. The massages were a splurge, but Nadia and Regan had been more than generous in giving Nic and Millie a free honeymoon. It was the least she could do.

Janice led them to the changing rooms. "You can leave your clothes and belongings in the lockers. You'll find bathrobes on the hooks inside the changing rooms, and when you're finished, the massage therapists will be waiting outside the door."

After changing, Millie met Nadia in the outer changing area. She glanced around to make sure they were alone. "Remember, pump them for as much information as you can. Obviously, they're spying on Grand Bay."

"Yeah, that snake Milner has been sending his spies to our resort," Nadia said.

"And we're returning the favor." Millie winked at her friend and they exited the changing area where two women stood waiting in the hall.

"I'm Telene. Which one of you is having the aquatic treatment?" Millie raised a hand and let out a sigh of relief that it wasn't a man.

"You're having the Amazing Azure?" The other woman turned to Nadia.

"Yes."

"Follow me."

The women parted ways as Millie followed Telene and Nadia and her therapist headed in the other direction.

It was an interesting two hours and by the time Millie finished with the water treatment, followed by the stretching and massaging, she was ready for a nice, long nap.

While Telene stretched and massaged Millie, she attempted to glean as much information out of the woman as she could. Unfortunately, Telene had only recently started working at the Serenity Spa.

"We are done here, but you can hang out here as long as you like." Telene leaned back. "Some clients need a few minutes to gather their bearings after the treatment."

"I can see why. It's pretty intense." Millie rolled onto her back and slowly sat. After a brief break, she made her way to the changing room and retrieved her belongings from the locker.

Millie slipped her clothes on, and then dropped the bathrobe in the bin near the door before stepping into the hall where Janice was waiting for her. "Did you enjoy your treatment?"

"It was better than I thought it would be," Millie said. She almost told the woman she still hadn't tried the Grand Bay Beach's spa, but figured the comment might cause the woman to become suspicious.

"Your friend is finishing up," Janice said.

The women chatted about the resort and the amenities sounded similar to those at Grand Bay. Nadia appeared a short time later, still wearing her robe. "I'll hurry."

"No need," Millie waved a hand. "Take your time."

Nadia joined them a short time later, and Janice led the way out of the spa area and into the main corridor. "Should I have left a tip?" Millie asked.

"I already took care of it," Nadia said. "My treatment was wonderful."

"Mine was too," Millie said.

The trio rounded a corner where a small group of people was headed their way.

Nadia let out a small choking noise, did an about-face and took off in the other direction.

"Is she okay?" Janice asked.

"I hope so."

"Maybe she decided to use the bathroom we just passed," Janice said.

"It could be she's not feeling well. I'll be right back." Millie hurried after her friend, who had disappeared inside the women's restroom. She shoved the bathroom door open and stuck her head inside. "Nadia?"

"I'm in here." One of the stall doors swung open and Nadia hopped out.

"Are you okay?"

"No. I saw one of our employees, Kelvin. He was wearing a Bayside Resort work uniform."

"You're saying one of your employees works here, too?"

"It appears so," Nadia nodded. "I figured he would recognize me and our cover would be blown, so I ran in here."

Janice joined Millie in the doorway. "Is everything okay?"

"Yes. Uh...I realized I needed to use the restroom. Guess it was all that jiggling around." Nadia scrubbed her hands in the bathroom sink and ran them under the hand dryer. "Sorry. I'm ready now."

The trio finished making their way to the front entrance. "Please come back and see us again," Janice said.

"Perhaps. Thank you for the tour." Nadia smiled politely and Millie and she exited the resort.

Millie glanced back. "That was a close call. It's interesting your employee, Kelvin, also works for

Bayside Resort. Do you think he's spying on you and reporting back to Milner?"

"Could be," Nadia shrugged. "It's certainly not the other way around. I had no idea he worked for our competitor, too."

"It's a conflict of interest, to be sure," Millie said. "What department does Kelvin work in?"

"He's a floater." The women stepped onto the sidewalk. "I know for sure he's worked the front desk and as a bellhop. We were short-staffed one week, so he filled in by mowing the lawns, all of which puts him in the perfect position to spy on us."

"And perfect for having access to say…the kitchen, the gas lines, not to mention the guest rooms," Millie said.

Nadia slowed. "Did you hear that?"

"Hear what?" Millie was having a déjà vu moment. "Let me guess. You hear footsteps again."

"You don't hear them?" Nadia shook her head. "I'm beginning to think I'm losing my mind."

"You have a lot going on," Millie said. "Cut yourself some slack."

"I'm going to have to, either that or check into the funny farm," Nadia said. "What if Milner is paying Kelvin to sabotage our business?"

"Motive and opportunity," Millie said. "How much do you know about Kelvin?"

"Not nearly enough," Nadia said. "But I'm about to find out!"

Chapter 14

Nadia headed to the office to research Kelvin while Millie wandered back to the cottage to grab her e-reader and change into her swimsuit.

Regan and Nic wouldn't be returning to the resort for a few more hours, which would give Millie ample time to relax by the pool and start reading a new murder mystery she'd downloaded.

Millie ordered an iced tea from the pool bar and then picked a shady spot near the back. She spread her beach towel onto an empty lounge chair and settled in before slipping her reading glasses on and firing up her reading device.

She quickly became engrossed in the mystery, about a young woman, Ciera, who had been adopted at birth. Ciera received an anonymous "to my daughter" birthday card on her 18th birthday. There was no return address, but it was postmarked from Atlanta, the same city where Ciera lived.

A second card arrived, this time a Christmas card. It was similar to the first, addressed to "my daughter," also postmarked from the same city...Atlanta.

Inside the second card was a clipping of a recent murder, not far from where Ciera lived. Soon, the young woman began getting the eerie sensation she was being followed and was horrified when she realized she was being stalked.

"I thought I might catch you down here."

Millie nearly jumped out of her skin and she clutched her chest. "Oh my gosh! You scared me half to death."

"Sorry. I didn't mean to startle you." Nic glanced at Millie's e-reader. "Killer Be Killed. It probably doesn't help, reading murder mystery books." He eased into the chair next to his wife. "How was the spa?"

"I enjoyed my treatment more than I thought I would." Millie told her husband about her aquatic yoga treatment and that Nadia chose something different.

"Did you decide to try the spa here?"

"No." Millie averted her gaze.

"You went to Marigot?"

"No. We tried the spa at Bayside next door," Millie said.

"To spy on them?" Nic chuckled. "Well, at least you weren't working on solving the murders." He studied her face. "You were?"

"Do I look that guilty?" Millie groaned.

"Only to me," Nic said. "I can read you like an open book."

"Great. Now you tell me."

"What did you find out?"

Millie told him how Nadia watched the local news footage on the internet and spotted Salvatore

Milner, the new proprietor of Bayside Resort, sitting in his golf cart, watching the resort's fire from the sidelines. She also told him how, when they got to Bayside, the staff all but admitted to spying on Grand Bay. "I view our visit to Bayside as an opportunity to return the favor."

"I see." Nic placed his hands behind his head and leaned back in his chair. "So it was a bust."

"Not necessarily. When we were leaving, Nadia spotted one of Grand Bay's employees, Kelvin. He was wearing a Bayside Resort uniform. He works at both Grand Bay and Bayside."

"It doesn't make him a killer," Nic pointed out.

"True, but it does make him a suspect." Millie set her e-reader in her lap. "Nadia said Kelvin is a floater. He's worked in maintenance, as a desk clerk and a bellhop. He has access to most of the resort and it wouldn't appear suspicious at all for him to be in any area."

"So you think the owner of Bayside hired this person?"

"Kelvin," Millie nodded.

"Kelvin, to sabotage his competitor by murdering several of the resort's employees and guests?"

"It does sound a little farfetched, but he has both motive and opportunity." Millie rubbed her thumb and index finger together. "If Salvatore Milner is putting Kelvin up to it, he's paying him big bucks."

"I guess my first step would be to look into Kelvin's background," Nic said.

"Nadia is already working on it." Millie changed the subject. "How was the golf outing?"

"A reminder that I'm old, out of shape and I need more practice."

"So you had fun," Millie said.

"Yeah." Nic slid off the lounge chair. "I'm going to go grab my swim trunks and take a dip in the pool."

"I'll wait here for you." Millie watched Nic walk away before returning to her story. By the time he returned, Ciera had been kidnapped by her stalker and the readers, along with Ciera, still didn't know who it was.

Thankfully, a hunky detective who was investigating the deaths discovered Ciera was missing and had started searching for her.

Nic dropped his towel on the chair next to Millie's chair. "Am I interrupting?"

"No. There's no good stopping point until I get to the end." She shut the reading device, covered it with a towel and wiggled out of the lounge chair. "All that relaxing at the spa and now I'm wound up tighter than a top wondering if Ciera's stalker is going to kill her."

"Ciera?"

"The character in my book," Millie said.

"Is it a true story?"

"No. It's fiction, but she seems real."

Nic reached for Millie's hand and they strolled to the edge of the pool. "You're the super sleuth. Who do you think kidnapped your character?"

"I don't know. What I do know is Ciera received her first anonymous card on her 18th birthday and then they started getting creepy."

"I'm sure you'll figure it out. Cannonball!" Nic leapt into the pool while Millie wandered to the steps and slowly waded into the water. Despite the blistering summer sun, the water was chilly and it took several moments for Millie to get used to the cold, but after she did, it was refreshing.

The couple swam and sunned for another hour until Millie's stomach started to grumble. "I haven't eaten since breakfast."

"Why don't we order pizza delivery and stay in for the rest of the evening, maybe take a romantic moonlit walk later?"

"That sounds wonderful. Let's grab our stuff." Millie wrapped a towel around her waist and they retrieved their belongings. She adjusted the beach bag on her shoulder and slipped her arm through Nic's arm. "You come up with some of the best ideas. Are we still going to explore the island tomorrow?"

"Yes. I think we should sleep in...take advantage of our non-schedule and then head out for the day. Regan suggested a restaurant in downtown Philipsburg, on the Dutch side. He said they serve mostly tapas food and I know how you like to try new things. I think it sounds perfect."

"It does. Maybe we can do a little shopping while we're at it," Millie said. "How is Alyssa, the employee who was burned the other night?"

"Better. Regan said he stopped by the hospital yesterday to visit Alyssa and she said she heard a hissing noise, right before the fire. The doctors are keeping her for observation to make sure there are no signs of infection. Depending on how her wounds are healing, they may release her from the hospital tomorrow."

"Does she plan to return to work?"

Nic nodded. "Yes. Regan said he was surprised. Alyssa had been dating Raoul, the worker who was found dead in the freezer and she's been taking it hard."

"Maybe she was so distraught over Raoul's death; she accidentally hit the gas line." When they reached the cottage, Millie dropped the beach bag by the door.

"You could be right," Nic said. "I'll order the food while you shower."

"I won't be long." Millie quickly showered and headed back to the living room where Nic was watching television. "The bathroom is all yours."

The pizza arrived while Nic was showering, and after paying the deliveryman, Millie carried the large pizza box, plus a smaller one to the kitchen counter.

She lifted the lid on the smaller box. The pungent aroma of parmesan wafted up and Millie's mouth began to water. She tore off one of the cheesy breadsticks and dipped it in the container of marinara sauce. One breadstick turned into two and by the time Nic emerged from the bathroom, she was working on her third. "Sorry. I never should've lifted the lid."

Nic wrapped an arm around his wife's waist and nuzzled her neck. "I thought I remembered you telling me breadsticks were one of your favorite foods."

"They are." Millie closed her eyes and breathed in the earthy musky smell that clung to her husband's shirt. "I love your new cologne."

"I bought it, just for you." Nic nuzzled Millie's neck. "And I love you."

Millie placed her cheek on her husband's chest. "It will be nice to relax and not do anything for a change."

"I agree."

While they ate, Millie and Nic discussed the deaths. "Regan doesn't think the police are looking outside of the resort for the killer."

Millie bit her slice of pizza. "Because he and Nadia are the prime suspects."

"I think you're right. They still haven't ruled out the husband of the second victim, the woman...what was her name?"

"Ellen."

"Yes, Ellen. Regan wasn't supposed to hear this. He has a friend on the police force and the friend said that the husband recently took out a large life insurance policy on his wife, right before they arrived at Grand Bay."

"What about the others?"

Nic shrugged. "Maybe he's trying to throw the investigators off...make it look like there's a serial killer on the loose."

"Could be." Millie plucked a slice of pepperoni off her pizza and popped it into her mouth. "I'm leaning towards it being either Salvatore Milner, the competitor next door, or Regan's former business partner, the one who's involved in a lawsuit. They both have motive and opportunity."

Millie finished a couple bites of her second slice of pizza before setting the half-eaten piece on her plate. "I'm full."

"That's because you ate too many breadsticks." Nic polished off his slice of pizza and chugged his water. "I say we put the food in the fridge and head out to the porch to watch the sunset."

"Another excellent idea." Millie closed the lid on the pizza. "You're full of fabulous ideas."

"Isn't that why you married me?" Nic teased.

"One of the many reasons," Millie shoved the pizza box in the fridge. "Would you like another bottled water?"

"Sure."

The couple wandered to the porch and slid into the rockers. The sun, a fiery flaming ball of orange, sank low on the horizon. When it reached the edge of the ocean and right before it disappeared from sight, Millie spotted a green flash of light. "Did you see that?"

"It's the green flash, an optical illusion."

"Cool. I've never seen one before," Millie said. "Did you still want to head down to the beach?"

"Sure. We can walk off some of our pizza."

This time, Millie remembered to bring a baggie to collect shells and during their walk, she found several to add to her growing collection.

"I'm ready to go back." Millie stifled a yawn. "I wouldn't mind turning in early."

"Sounds good to me." When they reached the cottage, Nic made sure all of the doors were locked and then headed to the bathroom. After brushing his teeth, he crawled into bed to wait for his wife.

Millie climbed into bed a short time later, and after saying their prayers, she snuggled close to her husband. Her last thought before drifting off to sleep was that she had married the man of her dreams and there was no way she could've asked for a better honeymoon.

The couple woke early the next morning and decided to eat breakfast in the restaurant before heading out.

"I wonder if we'll see Regan and Nadia today," Millie said.

"Regan asked if we wanted to meet Nadia and him at the pool bar for happy hour and to listen to live music. If you want to go, I'll send him a text message."

"Sure. It sounds like fun," Millie said.

Despite the restaurant being busy, the service was fast. Millie finished her second cup of coffee while Nic polished off his plate of pancakes. "These are delicious and a little different. I think they put vanilla in them."

"The food is very good. In fact, everything we've done and everything we've eaten so far is top notch. We need to make sure to put Nadia and

Regan in the Grand Suite when they cruise with us."

"I agree." Nic wiped his mouth with his napkin and dropped it on top of his empty plate. "We can catch a taxi near the front gate, but first I want to stop by the front desk to leave a message for Regan since he never replied to my text."

When they reached the main building, Millie waited on the bench outside. Nic was inside for several long moments. Finally, he exited the building and joined his wife, a grim expression on his face.

"What's wrong?"

"No wonder Regan never replied to my text. He's been in an automobile accident and Nadia is on her way to the hospital."

Chapter 15

Millie's mouth fell open. "Is he going to be all right?"

"They think so. We won't know the details until we hear from Nadia or Regan. I left a message, asking the hotel manager or Nadia to give us a call to update us on his status."

"Let's pray." Millie reached for Nic's hand and they both bowed their heads. "Dear Lord. We pray for our friend, Regan, that the injuries he sustained during his accident this morning are minor. We pray for those here at the resort who recently lost their lives. We pray for their families and loved ones and we pray whoever is behind all of these tragic events will be caught and no one else will be harmed. Last, but not least, we pray for Nadia, that you'll give her strength."

"Amen," the couple echoed in unison.

Nic squeezed Millie's hand. "I thought about heading to the hospital, but figured we would only be in the way. I say we wait and see what's going on first."

"I agree." Nic led Millie to one of the waiting taxis and they climbed in the back seat. "To Front Street in Philipsburg please."

Millie stared out the window as she mulled over the recent events. She had a sneaking suspicion Regan's automobile accident wasn't an accident.

There were too many incidents, one right after another. Who was behind them? She thought of Regan's former business partner, Wayne something. He definitely had motive, but where was the opportunity? Unless he had someone on the inside doing his dirty deeds.

Then there was Salvatore Milner, the owner of Bayside Resort. He also had motive *and* opportunity. It was possible the employee, Kelvin, who worked for both Milner and Regan and Nadia, was up to no good.

Millie still couldn't rule out Ellen Fulbright's husband, Gordy. He could have killed his wife and attempted to cover it up by making it look like there was a serial killer on the loose.

Nadia mentioned Gordy had an airtight alibi because his keycard hadn't accessed the room until late morning the day of her death, but Millie was convinced someone could've easily reached the second story balcony and gained access through the slider.

The fact Gordy recently took out a large insurance policy on his wife was suspect...not to mention the fact the killer took the time to pose Ellen's body, meaning he - or she - wasn't at all concerned they might get caught.

Millie remembered her cousin Gloria's favorite saying. "Always suspect the least suspect."

Front Street was bustling with shoppers and pedestrians, and it wasn't the idyllic waterfront village Millie had envisioned. There were people everywhere.

She waited on the sidewalk while Nic paid the taxi driver and then they meandered along the street, stopping often, when a store or shop caught Millie's eye.

Nic never grumbled or complained and seemed perfectly content to follow his wife around town. Roger always hated shopping, informing his wife it was a waste of time and money, that they didn't need any more "junk."

Millie smiled at the thought. Roger and Millie's Michigan home had been a sprawling four bedroom, three-bath house, with a full basement and a three-car garage, while Millie and Nic resided in an area of less than 1,200 square feet total and he hadn't said a word about Millie's purchases. Instead, he just smiled and offered to carry the bags.

"You're looking quite pleased with yourself," Nic said.

"No. I'm quite pleased with my husband. You haven't complained once about shopping, my purchases or where I'm going to put all of this stuff."

Nic chuckled. "That's because you're the one who will have to find a place for everything you're buying and I'm sure it will be the perfect place."

When Millie purchased as much as she dared, the couple headed to the restaurant Regan recommended and made their way inside. The cool air was a welcome reprieve from the oppressive Caribbean heat.

The hostess led them to a table for two near the back and Nic placed Millie's pile of packages in the corner before pulling out her chair. "Philipsburg is charming, but I much prefer Grand Bay and our private retreat."

"I was thinking the same thing," Millie replied.

Nic glanced at his phone for the umpteenth time.

"Still nothing?" Millie asked.

"Nope." Nic shook his head. "Let's hope that no news is good news."

The couple decided to try all new dishes and settled on sharing a tortilla Española, a Spanish omelet, also known as a potato omelet, gambas al ajillo, a garlic shrimp and jamón, queso y Chorizo con Pan, a ham, cheese and chorizo with bread, which ended up being Millie's favorite.

Despite sharing the dishes, Millie was full by the time they finished, and she'd seen enough of the busy shopping district.

"Should I buy you a portable shopping cart so that you can shop some more?" Nic teased.

"No. I'm shopped out." Millie stood. "You have to admit that I don't get many chances to shop when we're onboard the Siren of the Seas."

"Agreed." Nic scooped up most of his wife's packages while Millie carried the rest. Thankfully, there were two empty taxis parked at the end of the street.

"Would you like to tour the whole island or save it for another day?" Nic asked.

"Save it for another day, if you don't mind. We still have plenty of time, even if you spend the day at the golf tournament tomorrow."

"That is up in the air until we find out how Regan is doing."

The couple quietly discussed Regan and Nadia's predicament. The news of the automobile accident had been hovering in the back of Millie's mind all day. Now that they were on their way back to the resort, it was front and center.

Their taxi was stuck in some heavy traffic and it took twice as long to return to the resort. Millie let out the breath she was holding when they rounded the bend and the taxi entered the meticulously manicured complex.

Millie gathered all of her treasures while Nic paid the taxi driver and then reached for an armful of bags. "Shall we go inside and check on Regan?"

"Yes," Millie nodded. "I won't be able to rest until I know he's okay."

They strode into the building and approached the lobby desk. The clerk motioned them forward. "How can I help you?"

"Yes, I left a message earlier to speak with the hotel manager or Mr. or Mrs. Leclerc. My name is Nic Armati."

"Let me check the message center." The man shifted his focus to the computer screen and narrowed his eyes. "Mrs. Leclerc left a message and a telephone number for you to call."

The man grabbed a pad of paper and jotted down a number before handing it to Nic. "This is Mrs. Leclerc's personal cell phone."

"Thank you. I have Regan's cell number, but not Nadia's." Nic folded the sheet of paper in half and tucked it in his front pocket. "Is there any word on Mr. Leclerc's condition?"

"Yes. He was involved in a minor automobile accident and taken to the hospital as a precautionary measure. Mr. and Mrs. Leclerc are home and he's resting."

"Thank God," Millie gasped.

Nic thanked the man for the information and the couple exited the lobby. "I'll call Nadia as soon as we get to the cottage."

Back at the cottage, Nic piled Millie's purchases on the couch and pulled his cell phone from his pocket before dialing the number written on the slip of paper.

"Nadia. Nic here. The front desk gave me your cell phone number. How is Regan?"

"Uh-huh. Let me put you on speaker so Millie can hear, too."

"Hi Millie," Nadia said.

"Hi Nadia. Nic and I have been praying for Regan. How is he doing?"

"Regan is going to be fine. He's a little banged up and bruised, but already chomping at the bit to get back to work. The doctors told him to take it easy today, so I tied him to the chair."

"Ha," Millie said. "I would like to see that."

"Seriously, he gave me a good scare and a few more gray hairs. Thank goodness he was driving at a slow speed when he realized the brakes weren't working."

"The brakes went out?" Nic asked. "Were you having trouble with them?"

"Not that I can recall, but I don't drive the car often. A local towing company towed the car to an auto repair shop to check them out. We should have the car back first thing in the morning." Nadia's voice grew muffled. "What? Regan wants to talk to Nic. I'm handing him the phone."

"Nic?" Regan's voice boomed through the phone.

"Regan, glad to hear you're okay my friend," Nic said. "Perhaps we should pass on the golf tournament tomorrow."

"Not on your life. Nadia and I made a deal...I behave myself and take it easy the rest of today and she'll let me go to the golf tournament with you tomorrow."

"Are you sure?" Nic asked.

"Positive. I've been looking forward to this for months. I have some money riding on Spieth tomorrow. He's the best up and coming young golfer out there. I'd offer my caddy services for free to watch him if I wasn't so darn old."

"You're not old," Nadia piped up.

"Okay, advancing in my prime years," Regan said. "Nadia refuses to let me drive. Maybe the girls can give us a lift and then swing back by to pick us up later."

"That was part of the deal, Regan," Nadia said. "Are we still on for chocolate croissants and some shopping tomorrow, Millie?"

Millie's eyes slid to the mound of packages on the couch and Nic snorted.

She frowned at her husband. "Of course. I...uh...picked up a few things today while Nic and I browsed the shops over on Front Street."

"Well, I hope you still have some money left. They have a dress shop right off the Rue de la Republique I want to check out."

"As long as Nic is okay with it, then I would love to go," Millie said.

"Fine by me," Nic replied.

"Perfect. Let's meet up for breakfast tomorrow morning at the coffee shop inside the hotel lobby. We can grab some breakfast sandwiches before we head out," Nadia said.

"What time?" Millie asked.

"Is nine too early?" Regan asked.

"We'll be there with bells on," Nic said. "I'm glad you're okay, Regan." The couple told their friends good-bye and Nic disconnected the call. "What a relief."

"No kidding," Millie shook her head. "That could've been so terrible." She pointed to the bags on the sofa. "It'll only take me a minute to pack all of these away in my suitcase and then we can head out for a walk or maybe a dip in the pool."

"A dip in the pool sounds refreshing."

Millie made quick work of packing her purchases in her suitcase and then changed into her bathing suit.

"Ready?" Nic had already changed and was waiting on the front porch.

"Yep."

As they drew close to the pool area, the sound of steel drums filled the air. Millie spied a group of guests gathered off to one side. "They're doing the limbo."

"Do you want to join them?" Nic asked.

"Do you want to see me in traction?" Millie laughed.

"I guess we'll have to settle for a swim instead." Nic dropped his towel on an empty chair and jumped into the pool. Millie placed her beach bag and towel on the chair next to his and made her way over to the steps where she waded in the water and finally began swimming back and forth.

They swam several laps and then paddled around the perimeter of the pool. Millie was the first out of the pool. She settled into her lounge chair and closed her eyes.

She'd almost dozed off when cool water splashed her legs and her eyes flew open. Nic was standing over her, towel in hand. "Sorry. I didn't mean to startle you."

"It's okay." Millie patted her stomach. "I'm getting a little hungry." The smell of sizzling meat wafted in the air. "I think the cook hooks up a fan to blow the grilled meat smell on guests on purpose."

"An excellent marketing tool. Would you like a burger?"

"Now that you ask, it does sound good." The couple headed to the beach bar and climbed on two empty barstools.

"Hello. What can I get you folks?" The bartender, Jed, according to his name tag, handed them two menus.

"I've got this." Another man from behind the bar ambled over and slapped two napkins on the bar top.

"Whatever." Jed shook his head as he walked away.

Millie glanced at the second man's name tag, Favio.

"Something frozen and fruity sounds good," Millie said.

Favio snatched a cocktail napkin from the nearby stack and dabbed at his forehead. "I make a mean frozen piña colada."

"Sounds perfect, minus the liquor," Millie said.

"Make it two."

"Would you like to order something off the menu?"

"Yes. I'll have a burger with everything," Millie nodded.

"I'm gonna make this easy on you," Nic said. "Make it two, except hold the onions on mine."

"Two burgers and two piña coladas coming up," he said. "We make the best burgers on the island. You won't be sorry." Favio smoothed his man bun, and then slid to the other side of the bar where he reached inside the freezer and pulled out two tall frosted glasses. "I add a special ingredient my Uncle Sendora shared with me years ago. It's grown right here on the island."

"Oh really?" Millie asked.

"It's soursop, kinda like a sweet tart, but an actual fruit." Favio poured several ingredients into the blender, finished filling it with ice and turned it on high, watching as the mixture swirled inside the clear container. "That should do the trick." He turned the blender off, removed the lid and poured the thick liquid into the empty glasses. "Perfect."

Millie waited for Favio to set the frosty mug in front of her. She grabbed the straw and began swirling the creamy mixture before taking a sip. "This is delicious."

Nic tasted his. "I agree."

Chirp. Favio plucked his cell phone from his pocket and frowned at the front. "I gotta take this call. You need anything else right now?"

"No. I think we're good until the food arrives," Millie said.

Favio nodded and then sauntered to the half door. "I'll be right back," he shouted to the other bartender, Jed. "Gotta minor emergency to handle." He waved the cell phone he was holding and disappeared behind a row of shrubs.

"Odd man," Nic remarked. "I wonder if Favio knew the Fulbrights. Bartenders always seem to have an inside scoop."

Jed, who had been standing on the other side of the bar, wandered over and reached for a hand towel. "I couldn't help but overhear your conversation. Are you talking about Gordy and Ellen Fulbright?"

"Yes." Millie nodded. "We were wondering if you or the other bartender had heard of the recent deaths here at the resort."

I've been off for a couple of days and just found out this morning. I have a call into the French authorities since I think I might have some useful information."

Millie lifted a brow. "You do?"

Jed dropped the towel. "I shouldn't have said anything. It's probably nothing."

"What if it is?" Millie asked. "Does it involve the Fulbrights?"

"Yeah. Gordy and Ellen got into a big brawl the night before her body was found."

Chapter 16

Jed lowered his voice and leaned an elbow on the bar top. "They were both doing shots and then they started to argue. Gordy kept sayin' something about Ellen and one of the resort employees, accusing her of flirting with him."

He continued. "She was getting mad and kept insisting it was the other way around. Family feuds, they're not that uncommon in my line of work."

"I suppose not," Millie said. "I think the argument is still significant enough to inform the authorities."

"That's what I thought. I'm gonna do whatever I can to help Regan and Nadia. We're like family here and they're good people."

Before Millie or Nic could answer, Favio reappeared, accompanied by another resort employee who was carrying a tray of food. He set the tray on the edge of the bar and Favio reached for the plates. "One bite of this burger and you'll think you died and went to heaven."

"I can't wait to try it." Millie squirted a thin layer of catsup on the hamburger patty and set the bun on top before taking a big bite.

Favio was right; the burger was one of the best Millie had ever tasted. The French fries were hot and crispy with the perfect amount of salt. She gobbled her food, wiped her mouth and dropped the napkin on top of her empty plate. "That was delicious."

"I know my burgers." Favio reached for Millie's plate. "Are you staying here at the resort?"

"Yes," Nic replied. "We're staying in Castaway Cottage."

Favio let out a low whistle. "Top notch accommodations other than the owner's crib."

"It's very nice," Millie agreed.

"Not that I would know. Employees like me; we can't afford swanky digs like that. Tips aren't that great." Favio shrugged his shoulders. "You'd think if someone with big bucks could afford to stay here, they could afford to leave a decent tip."

Millie opened her mouth and quickly closed it, unsure if Favio was hinting for them to leave a tip or complaining. Either way, she shifted uncomfortably in her chair.

Nic must've thought the same. He quickly finished his food and placed the napkin on top. "We'll have to have another of those burgers before we leave."

The couple thanked Favio, hopped off the barstools and headed back to the lounge chairs to retrieve their towels and beach bag.

"That was an odd conversation," Nic said.

"From an odd employee." Millie nodded her head toward the bar. "What do you think about what Jed, the other bartender, said?"

"That the list of suspects is growing and the authorities have their work cut out for them."

After dropping their belongings off at the cottage, Millie and Nic walked to the beach and along the water's edge.

Millie thought about Regan's business partner. Wayne Clemson had plenty of motive, not to mention he had already proven to be a thief. It was the opportunity part that had her stumped. Unless, of course, Clemson had hired someone on the inside.

Salvatore Milner had just as much motive and plenty of opportunity. Still, would Milner murder innocent people in an attempt to ruin Grand Bay's business? She thought of the employee, Kelvin, who worked for Bayside Resort and Grand Bay.

Jed had said Gordy and Ellen Fulbright argued the night before her death and Regan discovered Gordy had taken out a large life insurance policy on his wife.

Her mind drifted to the victims. First, there was the employee found in the freezer. There was a chance he'd accidentally been trapped inside. Still, Raoul worked as a desk clerk, so there was no real reason for him to be in the kitchen.

Next was Ellen Fulbright who had been strangled.

Then there was the third victim, George, a longtime employee who was found floating in the koi pond. Millie remembered Regan mentioning George had left a message, asking to meet with him to discuss something. He'd died before Regan had been able to talk to him.

Alyssa, a kitchen worker and the fourth victim, was lucky to be alive. Millie made a mental note to find out if the investigators suspected foul play regarding the gas leak.

Then there was Regan's accident and the failing brakes. He could've easily plowed into someone head on and been killed.

"Ready to turn around?"

Nic pulled Millie from her musings and she nodded. "Sure. It has been a busy day."

"I agree. Would you like to head back to the pool and bar area to listen to music tonight?"

"I would be just as happy to stay in, maybe watch a little television and relax."

"Your wish is my command."

Millie took a long, luxurious bath in the Jacuzzi tub, and then joined Nic in the living room where they found a mystery movie to watch before heading to bed.

Tomorrow promised to be a busy day. Little did Millie know how exciting it would turn out to be.

***

Other than a bruise on the side of Regan's forehead, he appeared no worse for the wear and was in good spirits.

The couples chatted as they ate their breakfast sandwiches and sipped the gourmet coffee. Their plan was for Nadia and Millie to drop Regan and

Nic off at the country club and then head to Marigot to shop, followed by a stop at La Patisserie to sample the chocolate croissants.

If time permitted, Nadia planned for them to stop by the open-air markets, which were popular with cruise ship visitors.

"You're sure the car is safe to drive?" Millie asked.

"Yes. The mechanic who worked on the car assured me we were good to go," Regan said. "We drove the car home this morning and it appears to be fixed."

The country club's parking lot was full and Nadia navigated around several stopped vehicles before slipping into an empty spot. "Don't overdo it. Get out of the sun if you feel you're getting too much and drink plenty of liquids."

"Yes dear." Regan leaned across the seat and kissed his wife's cheek.

"I'll make sure he takes it easy," Nic turned to his wife. "Keep in mind how large our apartment is."

"I will." Millie waited until the men exited the car and then ran around to the passenger side of the car to join Nadia in the front.

"We have a slight detour to make before we hit the stores." Nadia glanced in her rearview mirror and pulled onto the street.

"We do?"

"Yes. Wayne Clemson is emceeing the golf event."

"Okay," Millie said.

"Which means there's no one at his office in downtown Marigot."

"What about a secretary?"

"Nope." Nadia shook her head. "I've been calling his office for the last three days to see if anyone answers the phone and the only thing I get is Wayne's voice mail."

"His office is empty because he's here at the golf tournament and he doesn't have a secretary or receptionist," Millie said. "I'm not following."

"I want to sneak into Wayne's office, to see if I can find anything linking him to the incidents at Grand Bay."

Millie said the first thing that popped into her head. "We could get arrested."

"I don't think so. It's almost a foolproof plan," Nadia insisted. "His office is in the same building as one of the shops we're going to visit. All we have to do is make a slight detour."

Millie had done her share - more than her share - of breaking in, but it had been cruise ship cabins and on a ship where Nic was captain. Visions of being tossed in a filthy French jail where no one spoke English filled her head. "I'm not sure about this, Nadia."

"I can't stand back and wait for the next victim," Nadia said. "We didn't mention it earlier, but the auto repair place said it's possible someone tampered with the brake lines on the car."

"Oh no." Millie's hand flew to her chest. "That's awful."

"Right," Nadia nodded. "I think Wayne is behind this. Depending on the outcome of the lawsuit, not only could he be sentenced to prison for theft, but also for tax evasion. My theory is he has someone working for us and that person is roaming the grounds, killing people or attempting to kill people."

Despite the alarm bells going off in Millie's head, she couldn't leave her friend in a lurch…and in danger. "You're right, Nadia. I'm not making any promises, but we can at least scope out Wayne's office."

Nadia tightened her grip on the steering wheel. "Thanks Millie. I owe you one."

"You may have to let me move in with you, because if Nic finds out we're breaking into businesses, he's not going to like it very much."

"And neither will Regan, but innocent people are dying and the business Regan and I spent years building is being destroyed." She turned the car onto a side street and pulled into an empty parking spot. "This is it."

Nadia pointed to the building across the street. "Wayne's office is over there."

Millie closed her eyes and said a quick prayer before opening them again. "Let's go check it out."

Chapter 17

Millie followed Nadia into L'Exception. The smell of leather, mingled with citrus filled the air. "This place smells expensive," she whispered.

"It is a little on the pricey side, but they have some beautiful outfits." The women perused the racks near the front of the store until Millie spotted the clearance racks in the back. The clothes were nice, but not worth splurging on since Millie wore her work uniforms most of the time.

Nadia caught up with her near the clearance racks. "Ready?"

"As I'll ever be," Millie groaned. The women exited the store via the back door that read, "la issue de secours."

"What does the sign say?"

"Emergency Exit," Nadia said. "Don't worry. It's okay."

Millie's armpits grew damp as she followed her friend into the alley and around the side of the building. Nadia pointed up. "I was here once, right before Regan found out Wayne was siphoning money and not paying the taxes. There's a set of stairs, leading to the office on the second floor, directly above the clothing store. I'm sure the door is locked, but if we hike up the fire escape, there's a chance one of the windows is unlocked."

"A chance?" Millie gazed at the back of the building and wrinkled her nose.

"Yeah. The window locks weren't functioning properly, so Wayne had one of the resort's maintenance workers stop by to try to repair them, but the building is old and they couldn't be fixed."

Millie shaded her eyes and studied the upper windows. Next to the windows and attached to the side of the building was a rusty set of metal steps. She lowered her gaze to the alley that ran behind the building. "I'm still not convinced your plan is foolproof, but if you want to give it a try, I'll stand watch."

"Awesome. We need some sort of signal, so you can let me know if you see someone coming," Nadia said.

Millie reached into her purse and pulled out her cell phone. "Where's your cell phone?"

"In my handbag." Nadia pulled her cell phone from her bag and waved it in the air. "The only people who might come out here are employees from the clothing store heading to the rubbish bin. I'll send you my cell phone number. What's your number?"

Millie rattled off her cell phone number while Nadia tapped her phone screen. "Got it. I sent you a message."

Ping. Millie's phone pinged and she glanced at the number that popped up. "We're good to go. Let's get this mission underway."

"Hold my purse." Nadia handed Millie her handbag and slipped her cell phone into her back pocket before scrambling up the fire escape to the second floor.

She tugged on the bottom of the first window. It refused to budge, so she scooched to the right, to the second window and gave it a sharp pull, opening it halfway. With enough clearance to make it inside, Nadia vaulted through the open window and disappeared from sight.

Millie jumped at a small rattling noise emanating from behind the dumpster. "I hope she hurries," she muttered under her breath, her eyes darting from the window to the alley.

The door to the clothing store flew open and a young woman who was juggling a stack of empty boxes, emerged. She gave Millie an odd stare and then made her way to the bin where she tossed the empty boxes in a compartment labeled "recycler."

She stared hard at Millie before stepping back inside the store and closing the door.

Millie turned her cell phone on and dialed the number Nadia had sent her.

"Hello?"

"Nadia?"

"Yeah."

"It's me. Millie. One of the clothing store workers dropped some boxes in the recycle bin and she kept giving me weird looks. You better hurry."

"I'm almost done."

"Okay. Hurry," Millie repeated.

"I'll be out in less than thirty seconds."

Millie ended the call and began tapping her foot as she stared hard at the window, willing Nadia to appear.

The store's back door opened a second time and a woman, this one older than the first, stepped into the alley. Her eyes met Millie's eyes and she made her way over. "Can I help you?"

"I. No." Millie shook her head. "I'm waiting for a friend."

"In an alley?" The woman lifted a brow.

Thankfully, the woman's back was to the fire escape because a sudden movement caught Millie's eye. Nadia was climbing back through the open window and the old escape began to creak.

Millie clutched her throat and coughed. "Ahem. Whew. Something suddenly got caught in my throat." She coughed louder. "I think it's your perfume," she croaked.

"Are you trying to tell me that I stink?"

"No, I mean. Maybe I'm allergic to French perfume."

Out of the corner of her eye, Millie watched Nadia nimbly navigate the fire escape ladder and hop onto the ground. She tiptoed around the corner of the building and then re-emerged, joining Millie and the frowning woman. "I don't know where the poor little pooch ran off to. Hopefully, he went home. You don't happen to own a small dog about this big?" Nadia spaced her hands several inches apart.

"No." The woman shook her head. "I've never seen a stray dog back here before."

"My friend and I thought we would take a shortcut through the alley and when we got out here, we realized it was a dead end, but noticed a small dog sniffing around your dumpster."

"Well," Millie reached for Nadia's arm. "I'm sure the pooch ran home." She glanced at her watch. "We better get going or we're going to be late for our lunch date." She dragged her friend to the back door of the store and they hurried inside and out the front door.

When they reached the safety of the sidewalk, Millie swiped a hand across her brow. "That was a close one."

"It was brilliant," Nadia beamed. "I never would've thought to start coughing to distract the woman. I would've froze, complete with the deer-in-the-headlights expression my face."

"It was legit," Millie cleared her throat. "You didn't get a whiff of her perfume?"

Nadia linked arms with Millie and they ambled down the sidewalk. "So it wasn't an act."

"Nope, although it may have been slightly over exaggerated," Millie said. "Now, you owe me a chocolate croissant and while we eat, you can tell me what you found in Wayne Clemson's office."

It was a short walk from Clemson's office to La Patisserie, where the line of customers snaked out the door and down the sidewalk.

The women joined the back of the line. "Are they giving food away?"

"No. Another cruise ship must be in port today," Nadia said. "You can always tell when cruise ships are in port. The downtown area and shopping district is wall-to-wall people."

"I bet seeing your beautiful island overrun with tourists gets old." Millie had never considered what the islanders thought when hordes of tourists packed their towns and jammed their streets.

"It does," Nadia admitted. "But it's great for businesses, like ours. We offer day passes, excursions if you will, to cruise ship guests. We make a little extra money while guests get to enjoy our pools, the spa and all of the other amenities. Many of our hotel guests visited our resort during a cruise stop and loved it so much, they decided to come back and stay with us."

"Ah." Millie lifted a brow. "So it's a love / hate relationship with us tourists."

"Yeah. You summed it up perfectly."

Despite the long line, it moved quickly. The women approached the bakery case and Millie peered at the selection of delectable, decadent goodies inside. "I don't see the chocolate croissants."

"La Patisserie sells so many that they don't bother putting them in the case, at least that's what I read online. I think we should both get two. I also recommend ordering a noisette. Noisette is French for hazelnut, the mixture of colors the espresso and cream make."

"Can I help you?" the clerk interrupted.

"Yes. We'll take four chocolate croissants and two noisettes." Nadia turned to Millie. "It's the French equivalent of the Italian macchiato. It's a shot of espresso with a drop or two of milk or cream and not as potent."

"You're the pro," Millie said. "I'll take your word for it."

Millie insisted on paying for the goodies and then followed Nadia out of the building to search for a place to eat their treat.

"I know a quiet spot we can enjoy our goodies. This way." Nadia carefully navigated the throngs of people crowding the sidewalks as she juggled their beverages. When they reached a shaded park area, the women wandered to an empty bench.

Millie eased onto the bench and set the paper bag between them before Nadia handed her one of the coffees and she took a sip. The caffeine sent a jolt through her. "Wow. This is some strong stuff. I normally don't order espressos, but this is good."

She unfolded the top of the bag, reached into it, plucked out a croissant and napkin, and handed them to Nadia.

"Thank you. Thank you for the treat," Nadia said. "I didn't plan a visit to La Patisserie so that you could pay."

Millie reached into the bag for a second chocolate croissant. "Nadia, you and Regan have been more than generous, inviting us to stay at your gorgeous resort, in one of your best cottages no less, and all for free. It's the least I can do. I can't wait for you and Regan to join us on the Siren of the Seas and we can pay you back."

Nadia nibbled the corner of her croissant. "I've never been on a large cruise ship. I've been on some of the island catamarans and fishing boats and they make me somewhat seasick, so I've always steered clear of large ships."

"If you're prone to motion sickness, I suggest seeing your doctor for a patch. Sometimes taking motion sickness medicine will work, too." Millie tore a piece of her croissant off and popped it into her mouth. The flaky croissant and drizzled chocolate melted in her mouth. "Oh my gosh, this is delicious."

"La Patisserie gets rave reviews." Nadia polished off her first croissant and then sipped her coffee as she waited for Millie to finish hers. "That was a close call, back there at Wayne Clemson's office."

"Yeah." Millie nodded. "I'm pretty sure if the woman from the store caught you climbing out of

Clemson's window, she would've called the police and we'd be sitting in a jail cell right about now."

"You worry too much," Nadia said. "Thanks to your quick thinking, it didn't happen."

"Thanks to the woman's overpowering perfume," Millie said. "I'm dying to know...did you find anything interesting inside Clemson's office?"

"Yep. Wayne Clemson isn't at the golf tournament today. In fact, he isn't even on the island and hasn't been for days."

Chapter 18

Millie blinked rapidly. "Wayne Clemson isn't even on the island?"

"Nope. His office was clean as a whistle. Of course, his office drawers and filing cabinet were locked. I was getting ready to climb back out when I noticed he had one of the old-fashioned answering machines and the message light was blinking."

"Curiosity kills the cat," Millie said. "Let me guess…you pressed the button and listened to the messages."

"Of course. One was from Clemson's landlord, threatening to evict him if he didn't pay his rent. There was also an automated message from the utility company telling him they were shutting off his power and the last, most important message, was from another former business partner who said he knew Clemson had "flown the coop" and took off for the States, that he was gonna track him down and collect the money he owed him."

"Maybe he left town for a couple of days," Millie said.

"I would've thought the same thing except the former partner said he was giving Clemson until the end of June to pay the money back, so who knows how long ago the snake left the island."

"Isn't he in the middle of a lawsuit?" Millie asked.

"Yeah." Nadia shrugged. "He doesn't have to be here unless he's been convicted of a crime and a judge prohibits him from traveling, which apparently hasn't happened yet."

"So it looks like we're down to Gordy Fulbright murdering his wife and trying to make it look like a serial killer targeting Grand Bay or Salvatore Milner, your competitor next door."

"It could still be Clemson," Nadia said. "I wouldn't put it past him to leave one of his henchmen on the island to carry out his dirty work. Based on what I heard, Wayne had more enemies than even I suspected."

The women finished their croissants and Millie swallowed the last of her coffee. "That should tide us over until later today."

"I agree." Nadia crumpled her napkin and tossed it into the empty bag. "Now let's do some shopping."

The women wandered through the shops and Millie was proud of herself. She only picked up a couple of small knickknacks that easily fit inside her purse.

The weather started to turn and afternoon storm clouds gathered. Millie eyed the sky warily. "We better head back."

"I hope the golf tournament doesn't get rained out." The women picked up the pace and jogged to the car. "I know the repair shop fixed my brakes, but I'm still worried someone tampered with them and will try again."

"That's a legitimate concern," Millie said. She thought about the fact her time on the island was more than halfway over. Would she be able to help her friends solve the unexplained deaths before she left?

When they reached the resort, the guard waved Nadia through. "It's our lucky day. There's an empty spot out front." She eased into the parking spot and shut the engine off.

"Thanks for taking me shopping." Millie climbed out of the car and reached back inside to grab her purse when something lying on the floor mat caught her eye. She picked up the small, round disc and held it up. "This was on your floor."

"What is it?"

"I don't know." Millie handed it to her friend and Nadia flipped it over. "It's blinking. Maybe it belongs to Regan."

"Or it could be one of the repair guys at the shop left it behind." Nadia dropped it into her purse. "We should meet up later for happy hour. We're trying out a new band tonight down at the pool bar."

"Sure." Millie glanced at her watch. "What time?"

"I've got to run back and pick up the guys at five, so I was thinking maybe five-thirty or so?"

"Sounds good. Do you want me to ride with you?"

"Nah." Nadia waved her hand. "I'll be there and back in less than half an hour. I've got some bookwork to catch up on in the meantime."

Millie thanked her friend for taking her shopping and for recommending the tasty croissants before making her way to the cottage. She placed her small trinkets in a larger bag and grabbed a bottled water from the fridge before making her way to the porch.

She thought about Wayne Clemson leaving the island. Maybe he was behind the murders and planned to use his absence as an alibi. The guy sounded like a shady character.

Then there was Salvatore Milner, the owner of Bayside Resort and Kelvin, the employee who worked for both Bayside Resort and Grand Bay Beach Club. Perhaps Salvatore had hired Kelvin to do his dirty work.

She remembered Nadia and Regan mentioning Kelvin was a floater and worked in several departments. No one would suspect him of hanging around the kitchen or the guest rooms, not to mention wandering around the grounds. It would also put him in contact with George, the maintenance man who was found floating face down in the koi pond.

Regan and Nadia had also mentioned George was anxious to talk to Regan. Had George stumbled upon something that might have led them to the killer or killers?

Next was Gordy Fulbright. Jed, the bartender said that Gordy and Ellen Fulbright had argued over her flirting with an employee the night before she died. Had Gordy killed his wife in a fit of jealous rage?

Still, it didn't make sense for Fulbright to kill his wife, especially after having a very public argument the night before her death.

The last victim, Alyssa, was still alive. Millie suspected the gas explosion wasn't an accident. Then she thought of Regan's accident and the brakes going out.

Millie slid into an empty chair and began to slowly rock back and forth. The only thing she could see that tied the deaths and other events together was the location. "I need someone to bounce all of this off of." She snapped her fingers. "And I have the perfect person to help."

She darted inside, grabbed her cell phone and returned to the porch. Millie scrolled through the list of contacts and pressed Annette's cell phone number, figuring she had a 50/50 chance of her friend answering since the galley would be in between meal preparations, not to mention the fact that each member of the ship's management had a limited number of cell service minutes available each month.

"Hello?" Annette's breathless voice filled the line.

"Annette. It's me, Millie."

"Don't tell me you stuck your nose in the murder investigations and now you're in jail and Captain Armati is refusing to post bond."

"Very funny," Millie said. "I'm not in jail. I'm sitting on the porch staring out at the ocean. There have been a couple more incidents here at Grand Bay and I needed someone to bounce my thoughts off. Do you have a minute?"

"For you, I have more than a minute," Annette said. "Whatcha got?"

Millie briefly outlined the list of suspicious events and deaths and then the suspects. "I feel like I'm missing something, that there's some obscure clue that ties the victims together."

"It's definitely not your run-of-the-mill crime, what with all those victims, near-misses and suspects." There was silence on the other end of the line.

"Hello?"

"I'm still here," Annette said. "Everything ties to the resort. The list of victims appears random, but my gut tells me otherwise."

"Me too," Millie said. "So maybe I need to take a closer look at the victims."

"That's where I would head next," Annette said. "So other than being up to your eyeballs in the mystery, how is the honeymoon?"

"Wonderful," Millie said. "Better than I ever dreamed. This place is gorgeous."

"Well, don't get too used to it. Andy is running around here like a chicken with his head cut off. I bet if you come back and ask for a raise he wouldn't bat an eye."

Millie grinned. "Thanks for the tip. Oh, before I go, how do you like the flowers?"

Annette grunted. "You know about the flowers?"

"Yeah. Cat told me Sharky ordered flowers Monday, before we left the ship."

"Sharky is driving me crazy. The man will not leave me alone. It's getting so bad, I'm considering slipping some ex-lax in a plate of snacks and sending them down to his office."

"Annette..." Millie said.

"I know. I'm not that cruel, but I gotta do something. People are starting to talk."

"I'm sure you'll have it handled before next Monday."

"You can bet on it."

Millie heard a muffled voice in the background. "I better let you go."

"Yeah. Things are starting to get a little hairy here in the galley."

"Thanks Annette," Millie said. "You're the best."

"Right back atcha." The line went dead and Millie smiled as she turned the phone off.

Deciding that a walk would help clear her mind, Millie grabbed the beach bag and wandered down to the water. Several guests frolicked in the ocean while others lounged on the sandy beach.

Still restless, she wandered aimlessly down one of the paved paths and found herself near the back of the pool area. Millie dropped her beach bag on an empty chair and made a beeline for the bar.

Jed, the friendly bartender Nic and she had met earlier, was on duty. "Ah. You're back. What can I get you today?"

"A nice tall glass of iced tea sounds wonderful."

Jed nodded. "It's a scorcher again. I thought it was gonna downpour a little while ago, but the rain clouds blew right over." He filled an empty glass with ice and then reached inside the fridge, pulling out a jug of brown liquid. "Your husband, he's not here today?"

"He's at a golf tournament with Regan."

Jed placed a paper napkin on the bar and set the glass of tea on top. "Regan is a good man. I hope they figure out what's going on around here. The guests, they're starting to talk, you know?"

"I'm sure they are." Millie sipped her tea and replayed her conversation with Annette. She absentmindedly began doodling on one of the napkins, writing down the names of the deceased and recent victims.

Raoul. Worked as desk clerk. First to die (freezer).

Elaine Fulbright. Guest. Strangled. Found in bathtub.

George. Groundskeeper. Found floating in koi pond.

Alyssa. Gas explosion in kitchen.

She tapped the tip of the pen on the bar as she studied the list. The feeling that she was missing something…something important, nagged in the back of her mind. Millie thought of the failing brakes on Nadia and Regan's car.

Jed abruptly pulled her from her thoughts. "At first, I figured there was some sort of love triangle going on with Raoul and Alyssa. I always thought Dennis should be a suspect in Raoul's death, but then after George died and Ellen, I don't know what to think."

Millie's head snapped up. "Dennis?"

"Dennis." Jed nodded. "He's in charge of the porters. He was hittin' on Alyssa, the same way he was Ellen."

Millie leaned forward. "Are you saying Dennis, one of the employees, was hitting on both Alyssa and Ellen?"

"Yep." Jed nodded. "He's on probation for it. He stopped by here last night and told me he heard Alyssa was out of the hospital."

Millie's eyes darted to the list. "Regan." The pieces of the puzzle began to slowly fall into place. She remembered how Regan and Nadia had mentioned a run-in with an employee who couldn't keep his hands to himself. Millie couldn't remember his name...was it Dennis?

The blood drained from Millie's face. "What department does Dennis work in again?"

"He's a steward. He carries bags to guest quarters."

Millie grabbed her list and hopped off the stool. "Jed, I think you may have given me a big lead in the murder cases. I've got to track down Nadia." She thanked Jed for the tip before snatching her beach bag off the chair and fumbling around inside for her cell phone.

Her fingers trembled as she dialed Nadia's number. The call went to voice mail. "Nadia. I have something important to talk to you about. Please call me back as soon as possible."

She remembered Nadia mentioning she was heading to the office to take care of some bookwork, so Millie raced out of the pool area and ran to the front lobby. "Is Nadia in?"

The woman behind the desk shook her head. "No. She stormed out of here, mumbling something about a tracking device."

"A tracking device?" Millie's mouth flew open. The small round cylinder on the floor of Nadia's car was a tracking device. The killer was after Nadia!

Chapter 19

"How long ago did she leave?" Millie asked. "Do you know where Nadia was headed?"

"She left fifteen or twenty minutes ago. All I know is she climbed into her car and peeled out of the parking lot." The woman started to say something and abruptly shut her mouth.

"What?"

"I'm sorry. I shouldn't have told you that," the woman said.

Millie took a step forward. "It's imperative you tell me what you know. Nadia's life may be in danger."

"Well, I think she was going to find Regan and confront him about what she found. I guess it was the tracking device."

"Thanks for the info." Millie jogged out of the lobby, juggling her phone in one hand as she dialed Nic's cell phone number. The call went directly to voice mail.

Millie left an urgent message, telling Nic to call her right away and then ran to an empty taxi, parked alongside the curb. She crawled into the back seat, slamming the door shut behind her. "I need to get to the Mullet Bay Country Club pronto."

"You got it." The taxi sped along the winding, island roads as Millie anxiously peered out the window. Thankfully, the golf course wasn't far from the resort.

The taxi driver careened around a sharp curve causing Millie to slide across the vinyl seat as her lap belt tightened.

"Sorry. I didn't mean to take the curve so fast." The driver eased off the gas. "We should be there in ten minutes, tops."

"Perfect." Millie fumbled around inside her purse and opened her wallet. "How much will I owe you?"

"Forty dollars plus tip."

"Whew." Millie shook her head. "I should be a taxi driver."

The taxi driver gave her a quick look in the rearview mirror. "The rates are standard for the island."

"Sorry. I didn't mean to complain." Millie pulled two twenty dollar bills and an extra five from her wallet. She shoved her wallet back in her purse and snapped it shut.

The taxi rounded another bend, and they sped past a park Millie remembered seeing earlier. Nadia had told her it was popular for birdwatching and was frequented by the locals.

Millie's heart caught in her throat when she spotted a familiar car parked on the side of the road. It was Nadia's car. "Stop! That's my friend's car."

The driver tapped the brakes. "You wanna stop here?"

"Yes. Please."

"It's your dime." The driver steered the taxi onto the side of the road.

Millie unbuckled her seatbelt and reached for the door handle. "Don't leave. I'll be right back." She sprang from the car and ran toward Nadia's car. The car was empty and all of the doors locked.

"Rats!" Millie raced back to the taxi and hopped in the back seat. She reached for her cell phone and dialed Nadia's number. Again, it went to voice mail.

"Nadia. It's me, Millie. I'm here at the park, parked in front of your car. Please call me to let me know you're all right." She disconnected the call.

"The car has a flat tire," the taxi driver said.

"It does?" Millie spun around and stared out the back window. Sure enough, the driver's side tire was flatter than a pancake. "How far are we from Mullet Bay?"

"Five minutes tops."

"Let's keep going. Drive a little slower in case my friend is walking to the golf course."

The taxi pulled back onto the road and Millie scanned the sides of the road for signs of Nadia. Her heart began to race and an overwhelming feeling of dread filled her. Someone had planted a tracking device in Nadia's car. Someone had tampered with Nadia's brake lines. Millie suspected someone had also tampered with Nadia's tire, the same person who was tracking her.

The taxi barely reached the curb when Millie dropped the money over the front seat and hopped out of the taxi. "Thanks for the lift."

"Good luck finding your friend."

"Thanks." Millie slammed the door and marched into the clubhouse, making her way to the sign-in desk. "Have you seen a tall, slender woman with black hair? She would've come in here less than an hour ago."

The two men behind the table both shook their heads. "No. We've been here all day."

Millie rubbed her forehead. "I'm also looking for Regan Leclerc. I think he's a regular here."

"I know Regan," one of the men replied. "He should be down on the ninth hole by now."

"Is there any way to contact him? It's an emergency."

"I can radio one of the tournament organizers to track him down." The man picked up a walkie-talkie sitting nearby. "And you are?"

"Millie San…I mean Armati. Millie Armati." Millie briefly closed her eyes, forcing herself to remain calm.

The man lifted the radio and began talking to someone on the other end while Millie prayed. She needed to get back to the park, to Nadia's car. If Nadia hadn't come this way, where had she gone. Unless...

Millie's heart skipped a beat. What if whoever had planted the tracking device, figured out it had been removed, so they decided to tamper with her tire, knowing it was only a matter of time before her car tire went flat, leaving her stranded and vulnerable?

"Mr. Leclerc and his guest are on their way up here," the man said.

"Thank you." Millie paced as she waited for Nic and Regan.

"Millie." Nic hurried toward his wife and Regan followed close behind. "The tournament host tracked us down; telling us there was some sort of emergency. What's wrong? Where's Nadia?"

"I don't know." Millie began rambling incoherently and Nic touched his wife's arm.

"Take a deep breath and start again. This time a little slower."

"I found a tracking device in Nadia's car when we got back from our shopping trip. After talking to the clerk at the front desk, I think she suspected Regan might have planted it. She was coming here to talk to you, so I followed her because I think I know who killed the people at the resort and tampered with the car brakes. They also tampered with Nadia's car tire. I think it's your employee, Dennis. He's behind all of this."

"Where's Nadia?" Regan repeated, a note of alarm in his voice.

"I don't know. I tried calling her cell phone but she didn't answer, so I took a taxi here. We passed her car on the way here. It has a flat tire and I think she's in trouble."

"I'm calling the police. Where did you see her car?" Regan asked.

"Near the park, about five minutes from here. Nadia told me earlier it's where the locals go to birdwatch."

"Let me try to call her first." Regan reached inside his front pocket and pulled out his cell phone.

Millie clenched her fists, silently praying Nadia would answer.

"There's no answer," Regan said. "The park you mentioned is Pelican Park. It's time to call the authorities." He tapped the screen and then held the phone to his ear. "This is Regan Leclerc. My wife's car broke down near Pelican Park and now she's missing. I suspect someone is stalking her and her life may be in danger."

"Yes. I'll meet you there." Regan ended the call and shoved the phone in his pocket. "We can grab a taxi out front."

The trio hurried to the exit and Nic stopped. "Someone needs to stay here in case Nadia shows up."

"True," Millie agreed. "I'll stay if you promise you'll call me as soon as you have any news."

"Absolutely."

Millie followed them to the curb, watched as they climbed into an empty taxi and sped off.

It seemed like an eternity as Millie paced and prayed, waiting for word. She thought about heading to Pelican Park, but remembered her promise to stay put in case Nadia showed up.

She checked her phone every couple of minutes, and was tempted to try Nadia's number again, but knew it was futile. Time dragged and at the two-hour mark, Millie contemplated throwing caution to the wind and heading to Pelican Park.

She was halfway to an empty taxi when she spotted a familiar car pull into the circular drive. It was Nadia's car.

Millie could see Regan behind the wheel. Her knees started to buckle when she spotted Nadia in the front passenger seat.

Regan pulled close to the curb and Nic, who was seated in the back, hopped out, meeting his wife on the sidewalk. "Nadia is safe. After her tire went flat, she tried to call for roadside assistance, but her cell phone battery had died, so she decided to walk into the park to borrow someone's cell phone."

Millie pulled the crumpled napkin from her pocket and waved it in Nic's face. "I...I thought something terrible had happened to Nadia. This list of victims. If you take the first letter of each person's name, it spells Regan. R = Raoul. E = Ellen. G = George. A = Alyssa. All that was left was an 'N' for Nadia."

She rambled on. "I was talking to Jed at the bar earlier and he told me something very interesting."

"Wait until we get in the car and then you can tell Regan and Nadia, too." Nic opened the rear passenger door and Millie climbed in the back. "I thought something terrible had happened to you."

"Lucky me. I managed to get a flat tire and my cell phone battery died," Nadia said.

"Nadia is terrible about keeping her cell phone charged," Regan added.

"I learned my lesson." Nadia shifted in the seat. "What's this hunch you have? You think you know who planted the tracking device?"

"Yes. I think it was your employee, Dennis something. Isn't he the one who was on probation for harassing female employees? According to Jed, he was hitting on not only Ellen Fulbright, but also Alyssa, the employee involved in the explosion."

"And Alyssa was dating Raoul." Nadia clutched Regan's arm. "Raoul reported Dennis."

Regan tightened his grip on the steering wheel. "You're never gonna guess who Nic and I ran into near Nadia's car when we stopped to fix the flat and found her."

"Dennis," Millie whispered.

"He told Regan he happened to be driving by and recognized the car, so he stopped to see if he could help," Nadia said.

"Follow me here. Let's say Dennis flirted with Ellen Fulbright. Maybe she flirted back. Gordy and Ellen argued about it at the bar," Millie said. "Maybe Ellen rejected Dennis' advances, so he snuck into her room and strangled her."

Nadia picked up. "He also hit on Alyssa. Raoul was one of the employees who reported Dennis' behavior to us. What if he tricked Raoul into going into the walk-in freezer and then trapped him inside?"

"Dennis tried to take out Alyssa, too," Regan chimed in. "It still doesn't mean he tampered with our car's brakes or planted a tracking device."

"It sure does," Nadia disagreed. "He was given his last warning. I never lock the car. He could easily have slipped a tracking device under the seat and I never would've known."

"Except that it must've slid onto the floorboard where I found it." Millie handed the crumpled napkin to Nadia. "This list. Take the first letter of each victim's name and tell me what it spells."

Nadia studied the napkin and her hand began to tremble. "It spells Regan. The only victim left is someone whose name starts with the letter 'N.' But why target Regan?"

"I don't know. All I know is 'N' is for Nadia," Millie said. "You were next. I feel it in my bones."

"Remember when you passed Dennis over for that promotion?" Nadia asked. "What if his plan was to either take you out or to frame you?"

"I don't know. The authorities were working on a search warrant for George's place," Regan said. "I think it's time for me to give them a call."

When they reached the resort, the foursome headed to the bar, so Regan and Nadia could question Jed again, but he'd finished his shift and left for the day, so they continued on to Regan and Nadia's cottage.

Regan left a message for the lead investigator, asking him to call as soon as possible.

While they waited, the couples discussed Dennis at length and the more Millie learned, the more she was certain Dennis was involved.

Chirp. Regan's cell phone began to ring and he picked it up. "It's the investigator."

"Hello Mr. Turbell. Thank you for calling me back. I was wondering if you've had a chance to check George Kobles' place yet?"

Regan grew silent as he listened. "I see. I have some information that might help you figure out what George was working on. It involves Dennis King, one of our employees. Yes, I'll be here the rest of today if you want to stop by." Regan thanked the detective and told him good-bye.

"Well?" Nadia asked.

"The only thing of interest they found in George's apartment was a notepad with his to-do list. One of the to-do items was to talk to me." Regan paused.

"And?" Millie asked.

"It said, 'Talk to Regan about a co-worker.'"

"He was onto Dennis," Millie whispered. "What if Dennis...in his sick, twisted mind...needed to kill someone whose name started with 'G?'"

"George," Nadia said. "Dennis must have been stalking George, too."

"The thought is so far out in left field." Regan turned to his wife, a somber expression on his face. "As much as I hate to say this, I think you were next."

Chapter 20

"Here's your glass of iced tea." Nic handed his wife a tall glass of tea and then eased into the lounge chair next to her. "I didn't know you were addicted to iced tea."

Millie sipped the tea and set the glass on the pool deck. "Not just any iced tea. Jed's special blend." She changed the subject. "Did you stop by to get an update from Regan on the murder cases?"

"Yeah, that's why it took so long for me to get back here. I ran into him near the tennis courts."

"What did he say?"

"They linked the tracking device found in Nadia's car to Dennis. The authorities questioned Alyssa not only about Raoul and Dennis' contentious relationship, but also about him harassing her. She remembers Dennis was hanging around the kitchen the night of the gas explosion."

"Jed can testify that Dennis was flirting with Ellen Fulbright," Millie pointed out. "The last link was George."

"The authorities are working on a search warrant for Dennis' apartment. They believe they'll be able to link him to all of the incidents and deaths." Nic slipped his sunglasses on. "You could very well have saved Nadia's life."

Millie thought back to the other day, when she spotted Nadia's abandoned vehicle and envisioned the worst. "Who knows what a crazed killer, bent on revenge will do. I read once that serial killers get a rush when they kill. But why Regan? Why would Dennis' victims spell out Regan's name?"

"The only thing Regan can come up with is he passed Dennis over for a promotion because of the recent accusations of sexual harassment. Instead, he gave it to someone else."

"So he decided to set Regan up, with the final victim being Regan's wife," Millie said.

"He appears to be a very a troubled man." Nic pointed at Millie's e-reader. "Have you finished your mystery? Did you figure out whodunit?"

"Of course. It was the butler."

"The butler?" Nic shook his head.

"I'm kidding," Millie said. "It was Ciera's stepsibling. When the authorities discovered there was a will and Ciera was the sole beneficiary, they went with motive and opportunity. Remember, in most cases there will always be motive and opportunity."

"Perhaps you should think about penning a murder mystery novel." Nic placed both hands behind his head and leaned back in the lounge chair. "The Siren of the Seas will be here to pick us up before you know it. Are you ready for the week to end?"

"It's been a wonderful week. I'm going to miss Nadia and Regan," Millie said, "but yes, I'm ready to go home."

The end.

If you enjoyed reading "Family, Friends and Foes," please take a moment to leave a review. It would be greatly appreciated. Thank you.

The series continues...book 12 in the "Cruise Ship Cozy Mystery" series coming soon!

Save 50-90% on Your Next Cozy Mystery

https://hopecallaghan.com/hope-callaghan-books-on-sale/

List of Hope Callaghan Books

Audiobooks
(On Sale Now or FREE with Audible Trial)

Key to Savannah: Book 1 (Made in Savannah Series)
Road to Savannah: Book 2 (Made in Savannah Series)
Justice in Savannah: Book 3 (Made in Savannah Series)

Cozy Mystery Collections

Hope Callaghan Cozy Mysteries: Collection (1st in Series Edition)

Made in Savannah Cozy Mystery Series

Key to Savannah: Book 1
Road to Savannah: Book 2
Justice in Savannah: Book 3
Swag in Savannah: Book 4
Trouble in Savannah: Book 5
Missing in Savannah: Book 6
Setup in Savannah: Book 7
Book 8: Coming Soon!

Garden Girls Cozy Mystery Series

Who Murdered Mr. Malone? Book 1
Grandkids Gone Wild: Book 2
Smoky Mountain Mystery: Book 3
Death by Dumplings: Book 4
Eye Spy: Book 5
Magnolia Mansion Mysteries: Book 6
Missing Milt: Book 7
Bully in the 'Burbs: Book 8
Fall Girl: Book 9
Home for the Holidays: Book 10
Sun, Sand, and Suspects: Book 11
Look Into My Ice: Book 12
Forget Me Knot: Book 13
Nightmare in Nantucket: Book 14
Greed with Envy: Book 15
Dying for Dollars: Book 16
Stranger Among Us: Book 17
Book 18: Coming Soon!
Garden Girls Box Set I – (Books 1-3)
Garden Girls Box Set II – (Books 4-6)
Garden Girls Box Set III – (Books 7-9)

Cruise Ship Cozy Mystery Series

Starboard Secrets: Book 1
Portside Peril: Book 2
Lethal Lobster: Book 3
Deadly Deception: Book 4

Vanishing Vacationers: Book 5
Cruise Control: Book 6
Killer Karaoke: Book 7
Suite Revenge: Book 8
Cruisin' for a Bruisin': Book 9
High Seas Heist: Book 10
Family, Friends, and Foes: Book 11
Book 12: Coming Soon!
Cruise Ship Cozy Mysteries Box Set I (Books 1-3)
Cruise Ship Cozy Mysteries Box Set II (Books 4-6)

Sweet Southern Sleuths Cozy Mysteries Short Stories Series

Teepees and Trailer Parks: Book 1
Bag of Bones: Book 2
Southern Stalker: Book 3
Two Settle the Score: Book 4
Killer Road Trip: Book 5
Pups in Peril: Book 6
Dying To Get Married-In: Book 7
Deadly Drive-In: Book 8
Secrets of a Stranger: Book 9
Library Lockdown: Book 10
Vandals & Vigilantes: Book 11
Fatal Frolic: Book 12
Sweet Southern Sleuths Box Set I: (Books 1-4)
Sweet Southern Sleuths Box Set: II: (Books 5-8)
Sweet Southern Sleuths Box Set III: (Books 9-12)
Sweet Southern Sleuths 12 Book Box Set (Entire Series)

Samantha Rite Deception Mystery Series

Waves of Deception: Book 1
Winds of Deception: Book 2
Tides of Deception: Book 3
Samantha Rite Series Box Set – (Books 1-3-The Complete Series)

Get Free eBooks and More

Sign up for my Free Cozy Mysteries Newsletter to get free and discounted books, giveaways & soon-to-be-released books!

hopecallaghan.com/newsletter

Meet the Author

Hope Callaghan is an author who loves to write Christian books, especially Christian Mystery and Cozy Mystery books. She has written more than 50 mystery books (and counting) in five series.

In March 2017, Hope won a Mom's Choice Award for her book, "Key to Savannah," Book 1 in the Made in Savannah Cozy Mystery Series.

Born and raised in a small town in West Michigan, she now lives in Florida with her husband.

She is the proud mother of one daughter and a stepdaughter and stepson. When she's not doing the thing she loves best - writing books - she enjoys cooking, traveling and reading books.

Hope loves to connect with her readers! Connect with her today!

Visit hopecallaghan.com for special offers, free books, and soon-to-be-released books!

Email: hope@hopecallaghan.com

Facebook: https://www.facebook.com/hopecallaghanauthor/

Bacon Mac 'n Cheese Bites Recipe

Ingredients:

12 slices thick bacon, cooked
1/2 box of elbow macaroni (about 8 ounces)
¼ cup milk
3 tbsp butter
4 cups extra sharp shredded cheddar cheese
Salt
Pepper
¼ cup breadcrumbs

Directions:

- Line a greased muffin pan with slices of precooked bacon.
- Bring water to a boil, add macaroni and cook for 8-10 minutes. Drain water.
- Add milk, butter, and shredded cheddar cheese, reserving ½ cup of cheese for top. Thoroughly mix together.
- Divide the macaroni and cheese between the cups in the muffin pan.
- Sprinkle with breadcrumbs and more cheese.
- Bake at 350 degrees for 15 minutes or until bacon reaches desired crisp.

Baked Apple and Walnut Tart Recipe

Ingredients:

1 – 8 ounce sheet of frozen puff pastry, thawed
1 Cortland, McIntosh or Empire apple, sliced and cut in ½-inch long pieces
½ cup walnuts, chopped
¼ cup brown sugar
¼ tsp cinnamon
½ tablespoon butter
3 tablespoons water
½ cup heavy cream
1 tablespoon confectioners' sugar

Directions:

-Preheat oven to 400 degrees.
-Melt butter in medium saucepan.
-Add sliced and cut apples. Sauté for five minutes.
-Add 3 tablespoons water. Sauté for another two minutes.
-Mix brown sugar and cinnamon. Add to apples. Stir thoroughly.
-Remove from heat. Add walnuts.

-Cut the puff pastry into four squares. Line 4 cups of greased muffin tin with the squares, allowing the corners to stick out.
-Divide the apple mixture among the puff pastry squares and bake until golden brown (20-25 minutes.)
-Let cook before removing from tin.
-While tarts cool, beat the heavy cream and confectioners' sugar with hand mixer until soft peaks form.
-Serve with tarts.

*Makes 4 servings.

*A special thanks to my friend, Cindi, for giving me some great pointers for an awesome apple tart!

Made in the USA
Columbia, SC
01 May 2025